SOUL TOLL

"In the deepest sense, you free yourself by finding yourself."
—Michael A. Singer, *The Untethered Soul*

"Lose yourself in doing all you must do to bring your soul life and sweet pools of light. Life, your life, is in your hands."
— Sarah Blondin, *Live Awake*

SOUL TOLL

For anyone who has ever wondered
if success is enough

A NOVEL

ANUSIA GILLESPIE

ISBN: 979-8-9993205-1-3 (paperback)
ISBN: 979-8-9993205-0-6 (e-book)

Book Cover and Interior Design: Creative Book Publishing Design

For my son, Raphael

Always, fight for your light.

TABLE OF CONTENTS

CHAPTER 1

THE COUNTDOWN BEGINS

The ballroom glittered under the light of a thousand crystals. Everywhere NP Dunn looked, the elite floated in black tuxedos and gowns in rich hues. Laughter rose and fell, buoyed by champagne and the comfort of wealth.

Dunn stood near a marble pillar. He placed his scotch glass on a high-top and adjusted the cuff of his tux, the loose gold bracelet at his wrist clinking with the motion. The sound drew a glance or two—exactly as intended.

Dunn had never cared for subtlety. Subtlety didn't put food on the table. It didn't keep the lights on. It didn't survive the hunger that clawed through childhood nights while men like these slept easy behind thick walls.

And yet, here he was. Among them.

"Quite the turnout," came a smooth voice beside him.

Dunn didn't need to look. He knew Roland's tone too well, always effortless, and amused.

Roland surveyed the crowd with idle interest, a half-smile playing at his lips. He was the kind of man who wore his tux

1

like a second skin, who didn't think twice about the price of the scotch in his glass or the fates of the men he funded. His life was built on the certainty that he could never lose.

"Think you'll make it to the finish line?" Roland asked, swirling his drink. His tone was light, but Dunn knew better. This wasn't casual curiosity, it was the voice of the man whose money backed the entire deal.

"Or is our little company about to become a humanitarian effort?" Roland added, smiling as though the outcome didn't matter much to him either way.

Dunn's jaw tightened, but his expression stayed cool.

"Twelve weeks," he said. "That's all that's left until this deal closes. I'm not worried." He met Roland's gaze, picked up his glass, and took a slow sip of his scotch.

Roland chuckled. "No? I've heard plenty of men say that. Not any who meant it."

"Maybe I'll be the first, then," Dunn said evenly.

Roland leaned in. "What makes you so sure?"

"Some of us didn't grow up with the luxury of failure," Dunn said.

Roland tilted his head. "Still carrying that chip, are you?"

Dunn turned back to the crowd, scanning the polished smiles and easy postures.

It was true. Roland had been born into silk sheets and gated estates, the kind of life where mistakes were softened or even erased by generational wealth. Dunn had been born into nothing. Every move he made was survival. And he'd learned early that survival wasn't pretty. It wasn't polite. It was brutal, and it required sacrifice—of ideals, of friendships, of anything that stood in the way.

Dunn's gaze landed across the room, and his fingers tightened around his glass.

James and Cynthia Brooke.

James stood straight but carried the unmistakable stoop of a man who'd spent too many years hunched over conference tables and glowing screens. His hair, once dark, had thinned and grayed at the temples. His suit was impeccable but hung too loose on his frame, and his glasses did nothing to hide the fatigue in his eyes.

Cynthia was radiant at his side, a contrast sharpened by proximity. Her crimson gown clung to her figure, the fabric catching the light like liquid fire. She laughed at something James said, genuine and full. But when her attention drifted beyond the crowd, there was distance in her expression—an awareness that ran deeper than the surface glimmer.

Dunn followed her with his eyes as she excused herself, slipping away from the surrounding guests. Alone, she paused near a small table at the edge of the ballroom. For a moment, she was still, the crimson gown pooling around her.

A camera flash popped—quick, bright—catching the moment and illuminating a glow at her heart.

A prickle crept across Dunn's shoulders.

He watched as she reached for her purse on the table, the careful movement of her hand as she retrieved her phone. One quick press of her thumb and she placed the phone to her ear and disappeared through a side door.

Beside him, Roland's smile curved just as Dunn pulled his eyes from the far side of the room. Roland tipped his glass toward the door Cynthia had just slipped through.

"Radiant, wouldn't you say? And receiving an award tonight from the Red Cross, no less." He gave a soft, appreciative whistle. "She does draw attention. She's practically incandescent."

Roland took a leisurely sip, then turned, this time looking directly at Dunn.

"Meanwhile, here you are." Roland's smile sharpened. "No spotlight. No entourage. Watching from the shadows. So, tell me, my friend—who's really holding the reins?"

Dunn stiffened. He didn't like having his power questioned. "I'll remind you that I am the CEO of this company. The deal's on track. Twelve weeks and you'll have what you came for."

"Let's hope it plays out your way. You know how... particular our terms are," Roland said.

Dunn smiled and waved a hand, as if dismissing the remark. But tension coiled beneath his skin.

His gaze lingered on the empty doorway.

They'd built the company together—Dunn, Cynthia, and James. The surveillance technology they'd developed was now worth millions, thanks in no small part to the capital from Roland's private equity firm. They'd scaled fast, pushed hard. And when it came time to sell, two offers sat on the table: one from the Chinese military, and the other from the Red Cross.

The China deal was worth multiples more—life-changing money. But Cynthia had refused, on moral grounds. And, as always, James had followed her lead. With their two votes, they held the majority.

Such an ethical pair.

They hadn't been willing to cross the line. When it came time to get their hands dirty, they'd gotten cold feet.

Dunn switched the glass to his other hand.

They started with enough. They could afford to be noble.

He hadn't had that luxury. And now, they stood in his way. Threatening everything he had built, everything he had clawed into existence.

But not for much longer.

He flexed his fingers and shook the gold chain down his wrist.

Beside him, Roland's eyes flicked to the movement. Roland shifted his weight, rising onto his toes and back on his heels in an easy motion.

"These things are good for the conscience, aren't they?" Roland said. And then, with a casual lift of his glass, he turned and wandered off into the crowd.

Twelve weeks.

In twelve weeks, with the Brookes out of the way, Dunn would close the deal with the Chinese military. And then— he'd be free. Free of investors. Free of doubters. Free of the old world and its old gods.

Tonight, the countdown began.

CHAPTER 2

HOTEL FOR LAWYERS

The office sat high in a brick-and-glass building overlooking Boston Harbor. Floor-to-ceiling windows framed the city lights shimmering across the water. Far off, the glow of a cruise ship drifted toward the open sea.

On the twenty-third floor, Ember Brooke sat alone at her desk, the only light in the room coming from the twin monitors in front of her.

Her name was on the deal, and tonight, that meant one thing: finishing the final review of a multi-million-dollar commercial real estate loan before the client's deadline.

She rubbed her eyes. The blue light from her screens stung.

The loan agreement sprawled across both monitors, its language dense and looping, clause references tangled like a maze.

Her phone buzzed against the desk, making her jump.

Mom appeared on the screen.

Ember answered. "Hi, Mom."

"Where are you?" Her mother's voice was warm, hopeful. Ember heard the rise and fall of voices in the background, and the clink of glasses.

Oh no, the Red Cross Gala. She had forgotten.

"I'm stuck at work," Ember said, bracing for the guilt-trip that would follow.

"Oh." A pause. "We really thought you'd be here tonight, sweetheart. We worked so hard for this award... and we were excited to show off our budding lawyer."

Ember's throat tightened. She leaned forward, elbow on the desk, forehead in her hand. "Well, sorry, Mom. In order to be someone worth showing off, I need to keep this job. And to do that, I need to be here. You know how it is. Please don't set impossible standards."

Her mother's voice softened. "I wish things were different. I wish you were here. That's all." She hesitated. "Will I see you this weekend? Maybe come by the house? We could work in the garden a bit. You used to love that... helped take your mind off things."

"I have yoga teacher training this weekend," Ember said. "Joy's leading some guided meditation thing. She mentioned a drum. You know me, I have to see what it's about."

Her mother chuckled. "Good. I know you like to peek into other worlds. Maybe keep an open mind this time. You might be surprised."

Ember smiled. "Okay, *Mommm.*" The familiar drawl softened the ache in her chest.

"Cynthia" – Ember heard her dad's voice in the background.

"I have to go, your father is calling me and they're flashing the lights for us to take our seats. I'm hugging you in my mind. Wish me luck."

"You'll hold the room in your hands, Mom. You always do."

"Love you, sweetheart."

"Love you too. Bye."

The call ended. The office silence pressed back in, heavier than before.

Ember let out a breath and glanced at the screen. The loan agreement still glared back at her. In the corner, a new notification blinked. She clicked it open.

An email from Brendan. Her old law school friend. The one person who could still make her laugh about all of this.

You still chained to your desk too? Misery loves company, thought I'd ping you.

Ember smiled.

Yes, shackled. Ember typed. *But I have coverage tomorrow. Yoga training, here I come. Sweet relief. What are you up to this weekend?*

His reply came fast.

Work. Enjoy the world without me! I'll see you in it again, one day.

Ember's fingers hovered over the keys. For a moment, she just stared at the screen. Then she closed the email and leaned back in her chair as her smile faded.

Law school had been grueling, but at least it was human, she thought. This was something else entirely. A "hotel for lawyers," the industry slang for Big Law rang in her head—places where partners lived on the top floors, and associates like her drifted unseen below. Days slipped by where her only contact with others was through a glowing screen.

She shook her head, pushing the stray thoughts aside, and turned back to her monitors.

The loan agreement waited, line after dense line. The cursor blinked, indifferent to the hour, the work, or the weight behind Ember's eyes.

She reached for her tumbler and took a sip. The water had gone warm, the taste stale.

Ember took a deep breath and straightened in her chair, her eyes narrowing against the glare of the screen. Hundreds of pages of dense legal language, and it was her job to make sure every defined term and cross-reference lined up perfectly.

She began her review.

Control F: "Property."

The keys clicked beneath her fingers, precise and methodical. Line by line, she checked each reference, confirming it matched the definition.

Control F: "Permitted Liens."

The familiar rhythm echoed in the quiet room, the only sound aside from the hum of the building's HVAC.

Control F: "Section 7.4."

Her eyes flicked to the screen. The reference was wrong. Section 7.4 didn't cover reserve requirements anymore, someone had edited the document and missed the update.

"Ha!" Ember said aloud, as she smiled. "Got you."

She updated the reference to Section 7.3 and saved her changes.

Feeling briefly accomplished, she paused, rolled her shoulders, then tipped her head from side to side, cracking her neck with two dull pops. And kept going.

Hours slipped past unnoticed. At some point, she glanced toward the corner of the screen. 11:08 PM.

Beyond the window, the harbor lights twinkled, the world outside moving on without her.

Control F.

The cursor blinked. And she kept going.

CHAPTER 3

A BREATH OF FREEDOM

D ing.
Ding.

Ding.

A gentle voice beckoned from beyond. "Open your eyes."

Finally, Ember remembered to breathe.

Having held her breath in anticipation, she exhaled.

Then, she then took a deep breath, her chest rising as she returned to life.

CHAPTER 4

WAS IT REAL?

A comforting aroma of incense and sweat permeated the humid air.

Ember's eyes snapped open.

Above her, a smooth white ceiling stretched, blank and sterile.

She froze.

What just happened?

Her fingertips gripped the natural rubber of her evergreen yoga mat. Around her, a dozen bodies stirred and stretched, lazy and unbothered—like cats waking from a nap.

But inside Ember, panic churned as her world tilted.

The cave, the mountain, the burst of light—the thrill and terror of it—all still buzzed under her skin.

Her heart hammered against her ribs.

The room swayed. But maybe it wasn't the room spinning. Maybe it was her.

She fixed her gaze on the ceiling, willing it to anchor her.

"Wiggle your fingers and your toes, bringing movement into your body," Joy's voice floated across the room. "Take your time. Roll onto your side to ground your practice. Then come up to a seated position."

Ember stayed frozen for a moment, the words washing over her. Then, trembling, she obeyed. Because not moving felt more dangerous than moving. Because staying still might pull her back into whatever she had just escaped.

She rolled onto her right side and stayed curled there in the fetal position, one palm cradling her face, the other splayed wide on her mat, gripping reality.

When she heard the shuffling of bodies around her, she forced herself upright, tucking her legs beneath her. She pressed her shaking hands deep into her lap, willing them to stay still.

Joy placed a delicate bell down beside her, next to a camel-colored drum stretched taut with sinew. Her dark skin glowed rich against the pastel lavender wall behind her, where the word "Breathe" was splashed in bright green brush strokes.

Ember glared wide-eyed at Joy. But Joy merely smiled, steady as stone.

The students sat in a circle on their mats, facing one another, some upright and alert, others still dreamy-eyed.

"Like waking up from a dream," Joy began. "Right now, you might be trying to remember every detail of your experience. Trying to hold on... trying to make sense of it. Or maybe not. Depends on what happened." She smirked. "So—what did happen? How was that guided meditation for you?"

Silence.

Not uncomfortable at first — but then the seconds stretched. And stretched.

Ember's heartbeat thundered in her ears.

Somebody, say something. SPEAK!

Joy waited, patient, a still point in the swirling quiet. Finally, she offered a bridge: "Let's start with this—does anyone here have a meditation practice at home?"

About half the class raised their hands without hesitation. Ember blinked.

You all do this alone? Willingly?

She tightened her fingers in her lap, the room stretching away from her like a place she didn't belong.

Joy smiled. "Beautiful. Now — would anyone like to share? How was today's guided experience, here in community, different from your own practice?"

The polished wood floor creaked as students shifted. A cough stifled into a sleeve. Outside, somewhere far beyond the heavy stillness, a siren wailed and faded.

Ember stared at the other students, floored.

How are they so calm?

She felt like she'd slipped into the twilight zone. An alternate reality. Usually everyone around her was on the same page, having the same experience, from the same place, of the same mind, the same sound, the same—the same.

Am I on the outside?

Ember watched as the only middle-aged man in the class stretched his legs out in front of him, the cuffs of his joggers bunched around his ankles. He looked like someone who used to care, before life wore the polish off. His faded T-shirt clung to a broad frame going soft at the middle. *Best Dad Ever,* the cracked white letters read. A relic from a life he didn't talk about.

"Honestly?" he said, dragging a hand through his short, thinning hair, somewhere between blond and gray. "I think I just laid there imagining golf. You know, the forest and all. Deep stuff."

He flashed a sheepish grin, and laughter cracked through the room that was too loud.

The laughter died almost as fast as it came.

Another classmate, the teacher's pet, smoothed an invisible wrinkle from her black leggings and then sat tall, the crown of her head practically scraping the ceiling. Her leggings and matching tank hugged a body trained for performance. A tight blonde bun adorned the nape of her neck, not a strand out of place.

"I visualized the trees perfectly," she said, enunciating every word. "Followed the path exactly. My cave definitely symbolized a threshold—moving into new stages of awareness."

She looked at Joy, as if checking whether she'd done it right.

Joy smiled and turned to the group. "Would anyone else like to share?"

Shilpa leaned forward, her cheeks plump and flushed pink. Her wavy hair was yanked back into a haphazard bun, loose curls escaping around her temples. She wore a baggy cotton top that was dotted with the residue of granola crumbs and looked like it had been slept in.

"Yeah, it definitely moved me energetically," she said, twirling a stray curl around her finger. "I didn't really see anything... but

I could feel it." She hugged herself and smiled a little too wide, the edges of it wobbling.

Ember sat motionless. Rattled. Scanning faces.

WHY IS EVERYONE ACTING SO NORMAL?

Brianna crossed her ankles, and Ember looked over – maybe New Age Barbie would save the day.

The hem of Brianna's cropped taupe hoodie rode up just enough to show off a sculpted, tan waist. Her mocha-colored leggings clung like a second skin, seamless and brand-new. Glossy dark hair tumbled down her back in loose beachy waves, tucked behind one ear to reveal a line of tiny gold hoops climbing up the cartilage.

"For me, it was just... pure peace," she said, her voice high and honeyed, every word floating like a bubble. "Like bathing in light frequencies. Totally aligned in heart-space." Brianna placed her hands with white manicured nails over her heart and then adjusted the drape of her sleeves and angled herself toward Joy. She offered a close-lipped smile. Her gloss sparkled in the light. Flawless, like everything else about her.

Still Joy said nothing, only watched them with that steady calm.

Ember stirred. She shifted restlessly on her mat, scanning the room, then did a double take.

Was this really happening?

Everyone had big beaming smiles as they looked to Joy for approval.

A beat of silence stretched too long. A yoga block tipped over with a soft thud, and *Best Dad Ever* leaned back on his hands, with a lopsided grin.

"Anybody else doing the math on how fast they could bolt for the door?" he said, jerking his chin toward the exit.

A few students laughed — not the belly kind, but the relieved, brittle kind that came just before something cracked wide open.

Ember pressed her palms hard into her thighs.

Around her, the others seemed wrapped in a dream she couldn't enter.

Joy smiled, unbothered. "These experiences can be intense," she said. "It's natural to want to know more, or to want to escape before you have to talk about it. As you process, consider this: Do you feel like you made it up? Or did it happen? Was it real?" She folded her hands in her lap. "And with that... I close class. The light in me—"

"No, we can't go yet!" Ember blurted. She leaned forward and planted her hands flat on the mat. "WHAT THE HELL JUST HAPPENED?"

•◆•

The studio seemed to shrink, the warm scent of sandalwood folding inward, trapping the heat and the silence between them.

Around her, a few students blinked like they were surfacing from water; others stared, wide-eyed, and one woman near the front just gaped.

Joy shifted her posture, angling herself toward Ember with a steady, unshaken grace. She rolled her shoulders down her back, unhurried. "You tell us, Ember. What happened?" she asked.

Ember pushed her palms harder into her mat and looked down to compose herself. She swallowed, and then looked up at Joy and held her eyes. "I was in a forest," she began, her voice steadier than she felt. "The air smelled like pine. The ground was soft... and then this hole opened up — like a cenote or a sinkhole, but beautiful."

Ember sat up as the words began tumbling out of her. "There were stone steps carved into the earth. I climbed down. And there was a boat — floating on an underground lake. It was tied up so I got in and released it. It floated, untethered."

A few students exchanged glances.

"It felt peaceful at first," Ember said, her fingers curling under her thighs. "Like... a real kind of peace. Like time stopped." She paused, searching everyone's faces, but no one spoke.

"And then I saw this purple triangle," Ember continued. "It just... floated in front of me. I didn't know what it meant. I didn't care. I just... was." She shook her head and covered her face. "But then something started pulling light out of me. From my chest. It hurt, but not the way you think. It was like... being emptied out." Her voice was now tight. "I followed it. I had to. And I saw — this prism. On a mountain peak. It was huge. Colorful light was trapped inside, darting around like it was trying to escape and that's where my light was going." Ember placed her hands over her heart. "I felt like I was dying. Like my soul was being pulled away from me."

She blinked at the group — at the polite, frozen smiles, the nervous shifting on mats. "No one else?" she said, her voice cracking. "You didn't... see that?"

Shilpa shook her head, arms wrapped tightly around her knees. "I didn't go anywhere," Shilpa said quietly. "I just... felt energy moving. No visions."

Ember turned to the teacher's pet. "You said you visualized the forest. You were there too, right?"

She pulled microscopic dust particles from her black leggings. "In my mind's eye," she corrected. "It was more... symbolic. A visualization, not a real experience. Right, Joy?"

Joy didn't answer. She only watched.

Best Dad Ever shifted, resting his elbows on his knees. "I wasn't kidding about the golf," he said, giving a hollow laugh. "But..." He hesitated, scratching the back of his neck. "I did see colors. Purples. Blues. Bright green. Not a prism. Just... floating colors."

A sudden thud — metal on wood. A water bottle tipped over and rattled into the silence.

A woman near the back murmured, "I had an intense experience too, Ember. For a second. But I didn't want to... freak everyone out."

Another voice broke in, unguarded. "I danced. Like — it was primal. And it felt like someone, or something, was watching."

The group shifted again, the illusion of control slipping, their bodies betraying what their words tried to hide.

Brianna, of all people, sat forward, and reached her hand out as a sign of support for Ember. "I saw the cave, Ember," she said. "And the boat. And when I let go... something pulled at me. Hard." She took a breath. "I thought... I thought if I let it take me, I wouldn't come back."

Ember stared at her. She was finally not polished, not posed, but raw and real for the first time.

Across the circle, Joy sat motionless, her palms open on her knees, her face unreadable.

The silence that followed was full. Heavy with the pieces that had just broken loose.

Joy let the quiet settle until no one dared shift their weight or clear their throat. Stillness pressed against the walls.

"There are thresholds we choose to cross," Joy said at last, calm and even. "And some that find us before we're ready." Her gaze moved across the circle, never landing for long. "Not every meditation is a metaphor. Some are invitations. Some are echoes." She folded her hands together. "The mind tries to make sense of what can't be explained."

She paused, just long enough to let the words linger and land. "And that's enough for today." Joy brought her palms together at her heart. She glanced at Ember, offering space for anything more, and then looked back to the group. "The light in me," she said, "bows to the light in each one of you. Namaste."

The students echoed the word "Namaste" in soft voices.

Then—clap clap clap.

Someone started clapping, and others joined in out of habit.

Students rolled their mats with practiced hands, looping straps with soft snaps. They tiptoed around the remaining mats and puddles of sweat that littered the oak floors, no one looking directly at Ember.

Ember stayed seated, her arms locked around her legs, forehead resting on her knees.

Joy stood at the doorway, nodding as each student passed.

Shilpa lingered at the door, her mat hugged tight to her chest. Her voice was low, just for Joy, as others continued to pass by. "Is there something I'm not doing right?" Shilpa hesitated, then rushed on. "That thing Ember described... I want to go there too. Is that something you can reach for?"

Joy looked in Shilpa's eyes. "You don't get there by wanting it," she said. "You get there by not pretending when it comes."

Shilpa's mouth parted like she might ask more, but nothing came. She just nodded, clutching her mat a little tighter, and stepped into the hall.

The last of them gone, Joy crossed the room and crouched beside Ember.

She rested a hand on Ember's shoulder — steady and warm. "Stay as long as you need," Joy said. "The door will lock behind you." Then she stood and walked away.

The latch clicked shut.

The studio had emptied, but the room hadn't settled. The late light sliced across the oak floor in sharp angles, catching edges of rolled mats and sweat-slick patches that no one had wiped up.

Her mat was cooling beneath the backs of her thighs.

Her body held in place, as if moving might break something.

Ember stayed on her mat long after the others had gone, staring at the door like something might walk through it, even though she already knew — whatever had changed, it wasn't out there.

It was inside her.

CHAPTER 5

EMBER'S SECRET

E mber knew in her bones that place—whatever it was—had been real.

But she wasn't going to say that out loud again. She wasn't a crystal-carrying, woo-woo girl. She was a serious person. A lawyer.

She hadn't gone looking for whatever that was, that world. She had stumbled in, an accidental visitor.

Still, something inside her had been unlocked. The cork had popped, and there was no going back to the way things had been before.

Ember vowed to keep her experience a secret to protect herself.

Who would ever hire a woo-woo lawyer, and a young blonde one at that?

"Oh god," she said aloud to herself as she cupped her face in her hands.

Absolutely not. She would not tell a soul. Her ambitions were too big for this unwelcome distraction.

Ember finally detached from her mat, moving to stand. Her body felt heavy, like she was dragging herself back into gravity. She forced herself upright and made her way toward the hooks and cubbies.

She pressed her lips together and pulled on her sweater, her coat, her scarf. Each layer felt like armor. The matte black pumps with comfort insoles went on last, toeing the line between elegance and readiness.

At the elevator, the doors opened, welcoming Ember to enter the harsh fluorescent light. She stepped in and rode to the ground floor.

It was Saturday evening, the fifth weekend of her eight-week yoga instructor training program, and Ember still wasn't used to the dissonance—spending hours moving and breathing in a warm, quiet room, only to be spit out into the chaos of the city.

The cold night air stung her cheeks. Smoke clouds floated above sidewalk musicians, and a man on a bench, half-hearted in his begging, transformed into a full performance as a swell of people rose from the subway station.

Ember tightened her grip on her yoga mat and threaded her way through the crowd, elbows nudging her as she wove between people wearing preppy jackets layered over thrifted flannel.

She could already feel the edges of herself starting to close back up.

Ember waited at the crosswalk, hugging the top of her yoga mat tight.

A silver CRV lurched to a stop in front of her, brakes screeching. The driver, window down, leaned out and shouted. "Oh, what the!?" His eyes bulged, wide with anger.

The shock of his voice slammed into her. Ember stumbled back, her mat slipping from her arms and unspooled across the tacky city sidewalk.

She dropped to her knees, gathering it into a floppy, unwieldy bundle. As she scrambled, she caught the man's eyes through the open window.

He jabbed a hand toward traffic. "If that guy had gone, I would've made the light," he snapped.

Ember recoiled, clutching the mat closer to her body like it might shield her. She backed away without answering.

By the time Ember reached her apartment, her fingers were stiff from the cold. She juggled the unwieldy yoga mat against her hip while digging through her bag for her keys. The mat threatened to unroll again as she wrestled with the lock.

Inside, she dropped her bag on the kitchen island and flicked off her heels, the clatter echoing against the high windows. The twinkling city lights streamed through the glass, casting a soft glow over the sparse but carefully kept living and dining room.

She grabbed her yoga mat by its edges and snapped it out like a beach towel, to then roll it tightly, properly. As she tucked the mat into its usual spot beside the couch, a glint caught her eye.

Ember turned, following the sliver of light slicing across the wall, her head tilting almost involuntarily toward the narrow shelf above.

"A prism," she whispered.

She lifted it down carefully, holding the glass in both hands. It was cool against her palms, heavier than it looked. A deck prism—gifted by an old boyfriend, one who had known her too well, too early. The memory pricked at her. She had thought it a strange present at the time. Decorative. A knickknack.

The glass had a mint tint, its angled facets catching stray beams of city light and scattering them in sharp fragments across the walls.

Once, on old sailing ships, these prisms had been set flush into the decks upside down, to bring light below without weakening the deck surface.

As she cradled it now, Ember's skin prickled.

A vibration stirred deep in her chest and rushed outward—tingling through her arms, her jaw, even her teeth—as if every fiber of her body was being called awake.

She was alive. She could feel that, now.

CHAPTER 6

POWER PLAYS AT THE FIRM

Ember carried her new secrets with her to work the next day. Hiding them in broad daylight since, of course, no one can look inside of her.

As she did every day, Ember entered the shiny white marble lobby of the tallest commercial office building in the city and hit "23" to call the elevator. She watched her coffee cup, always careful not to endure the rogue arm jostle from a fellow passenger, breathed a sigh of relief when leaving the elevator unscathed and marched to the safety of her office.

Back at her desk, Ember pulled up her calendar to see what her day looked like. Meetings from 1-3 p.m., perfect. She needed the breakup in activity. She didn't have the energy to "dupe" documents all afternoon.

David—senior associate on her biggest deal and son of the firm's Chairman, a legacy on the rise—rapped on her door-frame. "You ready?"

Ember nodded, grabbed a yellow pad, and followed him toward the presiding partner's office.

Jon had his Bluetooth headset on and was standing, legs apart, arms crossed over his chest, in front of his floor-length window. His voice boomed into the phone. It must have been annoying to be his office neighbor, Ember thought.

They stood awkwardly at the door, knowing not to go in unless invited. How could they make themselves known without making a noise or having any presence? If they didn't let Jon know they were there, he could stay on the phone for another 20 minutes, forgetting about his next meeting. He was too important for time, and yet his life was measured, valued, and determined by it.

They opted to step back against the adjacent wall and talk through whispers so Jon might realize they were there while maintaining power and control over the situation. They had not interrupted. He was still in control. He could then continue his conversation or invite them in. He did both—stepped into view through the doorframe and, with one hand pressing against his Bluetooth headset, beckoned them with a wave of the other.

They all took their seats. David and Ember sat in the standard, tired office furniture on the door-side of the desk, and Jon in his special, hand-picked partner chair on the window-side. In continued attempts to give Jon his space while physically being in it, David looked down at his phone and scrolled through emails, and Ember pretended to read previous scribbles on her notepad.

Every so often, Jon wanted their attention. He shifted in his chair or gesticulated grandly; they looked up. Jon then rolled his eyes, pointed at the phone, and grinned like they were all in the joke together. David and Ember mimed laughter, though they had no idea what they were laughing at. They all played a small game in the big cat's office.

After what felt like an hour of trying to busy themselves with old notes, Jon got off the phone.

Ember had met Jon a few times but introduced herself again to save him from asking. Then they got down to business. David ran through his status updates and questions. Ember was new to the deal, so she took notes and waited for information relevant to the documents she would be drafting. Fifteen minutes later, they were wrapping up. Ember thought Jon realized they hadn't exchanged any dialogue except for her initial introduction; he turned to her at what felt like the close of the meeting.

"You've worked on a mezzanine loan before?"

"Yes, several. I'm excited to work on this transaction with you both."

"Look, David will be a great resource and, if this doesn't work out, you can always try to use your law degree to get a job sweeping the floors at Burger King," he chortled.

Ember smiled and laughed politely. David snapped his head toward her and stared. She could feel his eyes. He was gauging her reaction. She kept her mask on, not quite sure what had just happened.

David and Ember left Jon's office and went their separate ways.

Ember walked deliberately toward her office, head down, eyes up to show deference while avoiding collisions. She heard the heels of a partner thwapping. The sound was approaching.

She raised her gaze to see a partner engaged in what could only be described as "partner swagger." This was her runway. Ember was her audience. She wore a short brown bob, a black tweed skirt suit with leather embellishments, and black leather heels with…metal spikes? Huh, that was a surprise. Ember liked it. Good for you—you've earned those metal spikes.

Ember hugged the wall and nodded politely to let her pass without obstruction. She saw the light of her office—safety—and hurried toward it.

Just as she settled in, David was back at her door. He acted like he was passing by and just popping in, but Ember could tell this was his destination.

"Ember, I wanted to check in quickly. I know you don't know Jon well yet—he's a joker. He didn't mean anything."

David studied her face.

"Of course," Ember brushed it off. "Please, I can handle sarcasm."

"Great," David nodded. He had done his duty. And off he went.

Why did he feel the need to assuage her? Was that interaction another building block for a bigger story? Ember could tell David was playing offense. Whatever, she didn't have the energy to speculate. She cracked her neck—one side, then the other—her shoulders rolling like she was shaking off invisible chains, and let it wash over her.

CHAPTER 7

WORDS OF SURVIVAL

Ember approached the hotel with enthusiasm; mingling brought a kind of spontaneity she liked. There were always new ideas to take home. After checking her coat, she made her way to the ballroom.

Turning the corner, she stopped. Frozen in place. A sea of blue suits filled the room.

Scanning from left to right, it was all the same: men in blue suits, laughing and patting one another on the back. Good 'ol friends.

Near the back stood NP Dunn, CEO of her parents' company. He was surrounded by a small group, listening while the others leaned in toward him. Ember recognized him from photos but had never met him in person.

Still, that circle felt far from where she belonged.

Only then did she notice herself—standing alone at the entrance, bag slung over one shoulder, doing nothing but staring. Instinctively, her hand found the strap, pulling it tighter. On a nearby counter, a tray of scattered cocktail napkins offered a minor distraction. She straightened them into a neat stack. Small order in the chaos.

Taking a deep breath, she stepped forward.

Introductions came and went. Names, titles, and sports talk passed around like appetizers. Ember nodded along, offering agreement when it made sense, until the huddle noticed her silence. To their credit, they tried to include her, shifting the conversation toward more general topics. Even that felt awkward, like her presence had nudged them off course.

The current speaker kept going, but Ember's focus drifted. Past his shoulder. A woman. The relief was instant. Ember excused herself and headed that way.

The woman was older, sorting business cards on a high-top.

"Do you mind if I join you?" Ember cut into the woman's gaze and gestured to place her wine on the table.

"Of course," the woman responded without looking up.

"Oh, Susan?"

The woman dropped her chin and looked up over a pair of gray reading glasses.

"Ember, right?" she said, removing the glasses with a small smile and a shake of her hair.

Ember nodded quickly. "Yes! It's so nice to finally meet you. I've heard your name for years. Growing up, my parents mentioned you all the time. Dunn's go-to attorney, the inestimable Susan McQueen."

"Ha, well, I wouldn't go that far Ember. You enjoying your time here?" Susan smirked as she gestured to the crowd.

"Ya, well. It's the world we're in, huh?" Ember said.

"That it is."

Feeling safe in her company, Ember took a chance. "I'm glad I ran into you today. Something strange happened earlier. Can I ask you a question?"

"You just did!" Susan couldn't help herself.

Lawyers.

Ember gave Susan the requisite smile and eye roll before entreating, "But really, I'd appreciate your perspective and discretion."

"Shoot," Susan encouraged.

Ember recounted the strange comment Jon had made about her ending up at Burger King and asked for objectivity, she genuinely wanted to know—was that something, or nothing?

"Ha, that's nothing," Susan said.

"Then why did my colleague come to my office afterward to gauge my level of offense? If it was nothing, that's the part that I don't understand," Ember implored.

"Look, I know law school was Disney World compared to the real deal. It's not your fault they didn't prepare you, didn't tell you how it is. Or maybe they did, but you weren't in a place to listen or understand." Susan paused before continuing.

"Either way, you're right—your colleague 100% came by to take your pulse and make sure nothing more would come of the interaction, which indicates that the partner was likely out of line. If your feathers had been ruffled, your colleague probably would have reported that up. The interaction wasn't 'nothing,' but in the scheme of things, relatively speaking, it's nothing. That's some lighthearted associate hazing. The guy probably thought he was shining his light on you and that you'd feel special for the rest of the day. You want my advice?"

Ember nodded.

"Don't get stuck on anything. Don't get negative, you'll only write yourself into a corner or, worse, dig yourself into an early grave. Women and minorities have been trying to change the system for decades and haven't moved the needle. You are starting to see things, and you will see much, much more. You might get angry, but don't let it fuel you and, most importantly: Don't Let Them See," Susan slowed for emphasis.

"This is the system you came into. Play by the rules. There are no shortcuts. Expend your energy working the system instead of trying to change it—I promise you'll be more successful that way. Look at NP Dunn. You think he got to the top by throwing punches? No. He smiles, and the whole room moves."

Ember confirmed her understanding and expressed her gratitude for Susan's candor. Susan's lips thinned into a line, and her jaw squared. With a curt bob of the head, she was on her way.

Now alone at the high-top, Ember grabbed her phone and checked her email to busy herself.

Ember, come back to the office. I need you for a deal. Thx. Rachel

She sighed and left the event without fanfare, quietly doing as told. Falling in line. She could do this, she encouraged herself, as she made her way back to the office.

Ember had passed the honeymoon phase of her job—the part full of energy and enthusiasm for the adventure before the mundane set in. Not even the mundane...ordinary could be beautiful and peaceful. It was the part where she was expected to know the unspoken and unwritten rules and abide by them. When she was expected to shut up, do as she was told, and just get the work done.

I'll be different. They'll see. I've done things differently before, and I've won. I'll do it again. I'm smart enough to figure it out. And, I will. Oh, I will.

Ember ruminated all the way to her office, and then her phone rang.

Caller ID showed Memorial Hospital—who died? She joked.

CHAPTER 8

THE CALL NO ONE WANTS

"Ember Brooke speaking." She answered in a low voice, as she always did since becoming a lawyer.

"Ember, this is Dr. O'Connor from Memorial Hospital. Your parents were in a car accident and we need you to come in now. Are you nearby?"

"What? Yes, I'm 20 minutes away. Are they OK?" Ember asked.

"See you when you get here."

"Hello? Hello? Are they OK?" But Dr. O'Connor had already hung up, and Ember was speaking to a dead line.

Ember ran the two blocks to her black Jeep Cherokee, set directions in her GPS, and raced to the hospital. Frantic, she parked in the drop-off lane and darted inside.

"Dr. O'Connor called me. He said to come in. My parents are here; last name Brooke. What room are they in?" She beseeched the nurse at the front desk, who stood to attention in pale blue scrubs, her dark curly hair pulled into a loose bun at the nape of her neck.

"Ember. We've been expecting you. I'm Nurse Dubrow, come with me." The nurse ushered her to a private room, and with the click of the door closing, turned to Ember, head down, hands folded.

"Please, sit down." She gestured to a beige chair with indentations and cracks in the brittle fabric; you could almost see the anxious people who'd waited here before.

Ember took one look at the chair and stayed standing, "No! Tell me what happened." Ember directed, with her arms crossed and eyes that urged the nurse to speak.

Nurse Dubrow removed her reading glasses, pinched the bridge of her nose, and then looked up to meet Ember's stare. She sighed, "I'm so sorry to be the one to tell you that...your parents, they were in a terrible car accident tonight."

"I know that part," Ember shouted in a whisper. "WHAT. HAS. HAPPENED?" She punctuated each word with the rise and fall of her pinched hand.

"Your mother passed, Ember. The doctor believes she died on impact."

"What? No, NO!" Ember's eyes widened as her vision shrunk to one point in front of her. The nurse's mouth opening and closing, the dreaded words tumbling out, over and over...died on impact...died on impact; her muffled voice sounded as if it were coming from under water.

Ember sat. She blinked. An ambulance siren screamed in the distance. *My mother is dead, my mother is dead, my mother is dead, my mother is dead.* Ember's world had gotten even smaller.

"Stop talking, I can't hear you." Ember raised a hand to the nurse and turned to the interior window. She had felt this once before, the feeling when the walls close in. *You're OK. You're OK. It's OK. Get out of your head.* Ember coached herself. She placed both hands to her chest to feel the rise and fall of her breath. To regain control.

Accustomed to the abuse inherent in her line of work—from doctors and patients alike—Nurse Dubrow did as told and waited in quiet compliance.

One hand rubbing her forehand, thumb to temple, Ember turned back to the nurse, took a deep breath and, on her exhale, gained the courage to ask.

"My mom. She's dead?" Ember's hand sunk down, forefinger resting on her upper lip with her palm hovering over her mouth, as if to keep herself from saying anything else horrendous. If you don't say it, it can't be real.

"Yes, Ember. I'm so sorry. And your father..."

"Dad? Oh my god, he's dead too?"

"No, no! Sorry. I was starting to say, And, your father, he's down the hall. I'd like to take you to see him now, OK?"

"Will he be OK?"

"Time really is of the essence, Ember. Let's go."

Ember cocked her head as she asked again, "That's not what I asked. I asked if he'll be OK."

"Dr. O'Connor can explain in more detail, Ember. Come with me, now. It's time."

Ember, knowing the nurse could not reveal more information, nodded in defeat.

Nurse Dubrow escorted Ember through a maze of hospital hallways, filled with beeping sounds, crying, and earnest conversations in hushed voices.

They arrived at her father's room. Nurse Dubrow opened the door, allowing Ember to enter first.

Her father was in bed with tubes and an IV for fluids, but he didn't look bloodied the way Ember had envisioned. He just looked like Dad.

"He doesn't even look bad. What's wrong? What's the diagnosis?" Ember asked.

Nurse Dubrow looked Ember in her yes. "What I can tell you is that he has internal bleeding. His prognosis is not good, Ember."

"Is he in pain?"

"He's on morphine so no, he shouldn't be in pain. We've done everything we can to make him comfortable. Now, it's time for you two to be together." Nurse Dubrow said.

"Internal bleeding…" Ember processed the information aloud. "So, he'll need surgery to stop it? Right? So what's the next step? Why is he just lying here?"

"We need to assess the extent and location of the bleeding and are waiting on the results of his ultrasound."

"How long? Time is of the essence, right?" Ember sassed in a failed attempt to produce results.

"Soon, Ember. Dr. O'Connor will be in shortly with an update. For now, just talk to your father. He can probably hear you." Nurse Dubrow smiled softly and left the room.

Ember sat in the chair next to the bed and held her father's hand. He gurgled guttural and jarring noises from deep in his throat. It didn't sound human, Ember thought.

Then his eyes opened wide as he lurched forward, choking out groans.

"Are you okay, Dad?"

Another nurse came into the room. The young woman, mid-20s at best, fidgeted with the machines, moved the pillows, and retrieved a bottle from the medical supplies next to his bed. She drew liquid up into a dropper and placed it on his lips.

"What's that for?" Ember asked.

"The gurgling. Sometimes it's hard at this stage for patients to clear the saliva from their throats; this helps." The nurse explained as she made notes on the chart at the foot of the bed.

"What do you mean, 'at this stage'?" Ember said.

"Oh, he's having trouble swallowing on his own. That's all I meant."

"No, you said, 'at this stage.' At what stage? What does that mean, exactly?" Ember deposed.

The nurse shook her head. "You know that I can't answer that question. Dr. O'Connor will be here shortly." She smiled to close the conversation.

"How can you be so cruel? My mother is dead, and my father is lying here and I'm the only one here to help him. But you've given me no answers, no prognosis, no timeline, nothing. All that I'm asking is what you meant by this stage—what did you mean?" Ember pressed.

The nurse looked Ember in the eyes, "At this stage, your time is best spent being here with your father. You don't want to miss these moments, trust me. At this stage, the kindest thing you can do is sit with him and assure him that you're here, you love him, and you'll stay with him."

The nurse gone, Ember sat there staring at her father, caressing the top of his arm, as he began to turn gray. She watched, feeling powerless.

"It's OK." Ember stroked her father's shoulder and kissed his forehead. She soothed. "It's OK, I'll be OK. You are amazing, Dad, and I love you." The tears came faster. She couldn't keep up the façade anymore. It was not OK. Nothing about this was OK. But she wanted to be there for him, just like he'd always been for her…in his way.

He groaned with a spastic movement of his left arm; the one Ember was holding.

"Oh Dad, are you in pain? Let me help you." Desperate to ease his mind and heart and discomfort, Ember pulled the sheets back to rearrange his body and find a comfortable position. She picked up his arm and dropped it in shock. It fell without resistance.

"Your wrist feels like an ice block," she whispered. Ember shuffled around to the other side of the bed and placed her hands side-by-side on his other wrist, squeezing to warm it up. She guided the arm to hug in by his side and tucked the sheet into his body for warmth before going back to the other side, also ice cold, and performing the same ceremony. With him sufficiently wrapped, Ember took her seat and caressed his face, the only portion of his skin still exposed.

His face grayed more; his jaw went slack. The gurgling stopped, which allowed Ember a second to think. She wanted to be with her dad again, to hug and hold and smile with him. To be alive with him.

"Hey Dad, remember when we went to see Van Morrison in New Orleans during JazzFest together? That was so ridiculous." She shook her head at the memory while wiping away tears. "Who does that with their college daughter? You always did things like that with me. We were so goofy." Ember reminisced as she burst with nervous laughter from a swell in her chest she could no longer contain.

"I wish we could Moondance right now, Dad. I had so much fun with you." Ember closed her eyes and went to that exact moment in time. It was Van Morrison, but somehow the lawn wasn't crowded. They had their own piece of the world with plenty of room to move and space to make silly walk-like-the-Egyptian dances at one another and laugh from deep within.

In that moment, Ember realized, they were free. Free to be present with one another, fully goofy, fully out of their heads and in touch with their hearts. That concert was the last time she remembered her dad happy. He was always so focused on work, calcified and grinding to make the money they thought they needed to then finally live life.

What about me? Ember wondered. *The last time I felt that feeling was….*

"On your boat in that mysterious cave, untethered." Her heart answered unexpectedly.

That can't be right, Ember chortled in disbelief. *That's not even a real place, it was just me lying on a floor in a heated room with a bunch of other wanna-be yogis.*

The door creaked open and Ember was pulled from her reflections. "Hello?"

A woman in full festival gear—flower crown, sunglasses perched on her head, and a vibrant, flowy dress—poked her head in. She looked out of place in the sterile hospital room.

"Hey! Just checking in on—" Her tone dropped. "Oh my God, I'm so sorry," she stammered, gripping the strap of her shoulder bag. "I think I'm in the wrong room."

Ember blinked, too stunned to speak.

Clearly mortified, the woman attempted an explanation, "I was just... visiting my friend down the hall. She had a... festival... incident?" She gave an awkward laugh. "Long story. Anyway, I'll just... leave. Sorry."

Just as the door was about to close, she popped her head back in.

"If it helps, he looks really peaceful," she offered with a kind smile.

The door clicked shut, leaving Ember alone once more.

Ember turned back to her father, to keep dancing with him, but he looked different.

"Dad, are you there? Are you still with me, Dad? Dad?!"

She placed the back of her hand to his mouth to feel for his breath, gauging time with her own. Even in this time of raw grief, simple breathing helped to center Ember. She waited for three breaths. For eternity. Inhale, and exhale. Inhale, and exhale. Inhale, and exhale.

He was gone.

It was dead quiet, now. Numb, she stood and turned toward the door. The hallway stretched out in front of her, and for the first time in her life, Ember had no idea what to do.

CHAPTER 9

MEMORIES

The sun hung low over the city, casting a golden hue across the rooftop garden, where friends, family, and colleagues gathered to celebrate the lives of Ember's parents. Laughter mingled with the gentle clink of wine glasses, as people shared stories and reminisced about the couple.

Photos were displayed on elegant stands among impressive bouquets of orchids, roses, and peonies—showcasing James and Cynthia Brooke dancing at galas and embracing friends at charity events, their smiles wide and toothy. In the center of it all, their matching urns sat side by side on a polished table, surrounded by the memories of their lives.

Ember's gaze shifted toward the back, where her parents' former boss and CEO towered, flanked by what appeared to be his usual entourage. He scanned the crowd with a faint smile, yet his eyes seemed to search for something more. Ember's stomach twisted, there was something unsettling about how he watched, as if he held a hidden ledger of their lives.

Wishing to extinguish the discomforting feeling, and simultaneously dodge more small talk and the constant refrain of

"I'm so sorry for your loss," Ember headed towards the photos, looking to busy herself in their memories.

She paused in front of a photo of her mother alone at a charity gala, framed in a glittering golden border. Her mother was in a stunning crimson gown with the fabric flowing around her like liquid, as she enjoyed a small moment to herself. Ember leaned closer into the photo and touched her mother's heart, where there was an odd light. Is that the flash of the camera?

"Hi, Ember." A voice cut through her reverie, making Ember jolt. She turned to see the tall man from the corner. He had broad shoulders, a square jaw, and a thick mane of salt-and-pepper hair. His weathered skin bore the marks of experience. Dressed in a tailored black suit, a white and gray checkered shirt adorned with golden cufflinks, and a shiny black tie, he exuded polish and confidence. Despite his powerful presence, though, Ember sensed a lingering desire for the spotlight, as if he had always aspired to be the quarterback, but never quite made it.

"I'm NP Dunn. It's great to finally meet you. I'm so sorry it's in these circumstances."

"Yes, me too. Thank you for organizing this Celebration of Life. It's beautiful. I was so overwhelmed and didn't know where to start."

"I'm very happy to help, is there anything else I can do? How are you managing?"

"Perhaps it's crass, but I've thrown myself into my work. Achievement feels good, and that helps right now."

"Your parents were so proud of you. Lawyer, right?"

"Yes, at Smith & Gray. Associate working my way up to partner."

"No wonder they were always talking about you. Good for you. Your parents were like family to me, and I will miss them dearly. I can't imagine your grief. I only wish I could have helped them more while they were still with us."

"What do you mean? They always talked about the most amazing opportunities with you. I'm sure you helped them a lot."

"Yes," Dunn began, and placed his hand on Ember's arm as he leaned in closer, his piercing eyes seeming to make a point. "But they just didn't quite make it fast enough, did they?"

Ember pulled back.

"You'll do better. Stay focused." Dunn advised as he turned the barrel on a sleek black and white striped twist-pen, with the tip extending and retracting with each turn.

Ember eyed the pen. "Is that from the guest book?"

"Oh, it must be. Bad habit." He wagged the pen, "I must always have a pen in my hand."

"I'll put it back so people can sign." Ember put her hand out. Dunn studied her with his head cocked, and as he dropped the pen into her palm, his exposed wrist revealed a gold chain. Each slightly oversized link formed a chunky bracelet that hung loosely, clinking softly as he moved.

Ember shivered. Dunn shrugged and sauntered back to his entourage.

Ember's gaze followed Dunn, his gold chain glinting under the fading sunlight. She shook her head, trying to rid herself of the strange tension he left in his wake.

As she turned back toward the photos, a familiar voice pulled her from her thoughts.

"Ember, there you are." Brendan's voice was warm. He was dressed in a tailored navy suit, his tie slightly loosened—a look that suggested he'd come straight from work. "I was looking for you." He was holding two glasses of red wine and extended one toward her. "You look like you could use this."

Ember blinked, surprised but grateful. "Brendan. You came."

"Of course." He handed her the glass. "How are you holding up?" His sharp eyes—honed from years of law school debates—searched her for the real answer.

Ember hesitated, her fingers wrapping around the stem of the glass. "Honestly? I'm not sure. It doesn't feel real."

Brendan nodded, giving her a moment before pointing toward NP Dunn. "I saw you talking to that guy—the one who looks like he's never had a bad day in his life. Was that Dunn?"

She let out a breath that was almost a laugh. "That's him. My parents' old boss. He's... something."

"Let me guess." Brendan tilted his head, his tone wry. "Big handshake. Talks *at* you instead of *to* you. Gives unsolicited advice wrapped in thinly veiled condescension?"

"That's disturbingly accurate." Ember sipped her wine, the bitterness grounding her. "He told me to 'stay focused'—like my career is the only thing that matters now that my parents are gone. It was just... weird. And he had taken the guest book pen."

Brendan frowned. "He stole the pen?"

"Not really. He just had it. And there's this photo of my mom—look at this. Her heart looks like it's glowing. What do you think?"

Brendan squinted at the picture, his brows knitting together. "It's probably just the lighting, but... it's kind of beautiful, isn't it? Maybe it's a sign."

"A sign of what?"

"That she's still with you, in some way." Brendan shrugged, offering her a reassuring smile. "You know I'm not into woo-woo stuff, but sometimes... it's OK to let things mean something."

Ember studied the photo again, her expression softening. "Maybe." She flung her hands up into the air, exasperated with herself. "Ugh, this is why I only invited you. I didn't want to have to keep up a pretense or explain these thoughts. I can't find normal. Everything feels off."

Brendan's expression softened. "Ember, you've been through hell. It's normal for things to feel off, even mess with your head. Don't overthink it right now—just give yourself space to process. You don't have to solve every puzzle tonight."

She nodded, her shoulders loosening. "Maybe you're right."

"Of course, I am." Brendan smiled. He straightened up. "Anyway, if you need a break from the intensity, I'll be over by the bar, keeping the wine company. Just say the word."

She nodded, her shoulders loosening slightly. "Thanks, Brendan. I'll catch you in a bit."

He gave her a friendly squeeze on the shoulder before slipping into the crowd. With a wine glass in one hand and the pen still in the other, Ember turned and made her way toward the guest book.

Ember stroked the pages of the guest book, running her fingers over the indentations of people's final words to her parents. Their final remembrances. Final feelings. She lay the pen in the tray, and turned the pages, absorbing the weight of the moment.

"Excuse me, may I sign?"

Ember turned to see Susan.

"Oh Ember, I'm sorry. I didn't mean to interrupt you. I'll come back." Susan was happy with the excuse to move on.

"No, wait. Don't go. Sit with me for a minute?"

"Of course, Ember."

As they walked, Ember noticed a delicate gold necklace resting just above Susan's collarbones. It suited her—unobtrusive, but intentional. They found two white Chiavari chairs just past the entrance, perfectly positioned to take in everything and everyone. It was the ideal wallflower station, a place to watch and listen without being seen or heard, where one could simply exist without the need to engage—a voyeur's paradise.

They sat in silence, Susan taking her cues from Ember. They watched the crowd—most moved easily, lightly. For them, this was but a drop of water on their life experience, a ripple that will have made its way through them by the end of the week. But not for Ember. For her, this was eternal. Forever. Final. A before, and an after.

A gentle breeze swept through, carrying the fragrance of roses that pulled Ember out of her head and back into the moment. The scent sparked something, prompting her to speak.

"What's the deal with Dunn, Susan?"

"I'm not sure what you mean, but he's known your parents for a long time. I'm sure he's just having a hard time."

"Hmm." Ember paused. "He said my parents didn't make it fast enough. What does that mean?"

"Oh, Ember," Susan replied casually, "they've always had grand ambitions. I think he just meant they wanted to reach the next level, and, well, that didn't happen for them."

"What a strange thing to say at a memorial."

"Maybe," Susan shrugged, trying to keep the mood light. "Or maybe not. Success was important to them, so it makes sense to talk about what mattered to them."

"I guess. But then he told me to stay focused, like it's my job to do better than they did." Ember turned to Susan. "It felt so off. Just weird. What am I missing?"

"Ember, he's my client. You know it's a gray area for me to even talk about him. There's nothing to find. You're not missing anything—just your parents. Grief can really warp your perception. I'm sure Dunn was just trying to mentor you, helping you focus on your success, your own oxygen mask, while you navigate your loss. It's not bad advice."

Ember took a deep breath.

"You OK?"

"Yeah, I'm OK. Thanks Susan."

"Alright. I need to go say hello to Dunn before the memorial ends. I'll be right over there." She pointed to a nearby seating area with oversized burgundy armchairs. Corporate men and women, polished and stylish, mingled around NP Dunn, who stood in the corner with a small, troll-like man beside him, his bulbous nose and deep-set, beady eyes giving him an unsettling appearance.

Ember nodded and folded her hands in her lap.

•◆•

With that permission, Susan stood and crossed the room to get her face time with NP Dunn.

She shook his hand and sidled up next to him, keeping it casual.

"Do we have a problem?" Dunn asked, smiling at the crowd.

"I never bring you problems, Dunn. Only solutions. You know that." Whether it was a room, a client, or an angle, Susan was always working. "What did you say to her, NP? She's spooked."

"I just told her to stay focused," Dunn said, flicking his hand in a casual wave that dismissed the question more than answered it. "Did you see the photos over there?"

"No, why?" Susan asked.

"Some idiot used a photo of Cynthia from the Red Cross gala," Dunn said. "You know the one. Ember saw it; I could tell from her face. She recognized something."

The troll beside Dunn piped up, "Need me to do something about it, boss?"

"No, not for this one. This isn't a job for you, Hector." Dunn's gaze followed Ember as she walked back over to the photos. "Ember's ambition is stronger than Cynthia's. She'll snuff out her light on her own, but she may need some reminders."

Dunn turned to Susan. "She trusts you. It's now your job to keep an eye on her."

"I'll keep an eye on her," Susan said, folding her arms. "But what's Roland going to say if Ember starts asking questions? You know that Roland watches the numbers *and* the names."

Dunn's jaw flexed as he adjusted the cuff of his shirt. "Let me worry about Roland. You just make sure her nose stays to the grindstone. You understand?"

Susan nodded. "Got it. But if she starts talking about any crazy woo-woo stuff like Cynthia did, I'm calling in backup." She rolled her eyes. "You know I can't keep a straight face with that nonsense."

Dunn chuckled. "What, you don't want to clear our chakras together?"

Hector grunted. "I'll bring the sage." His voice was gruff and gravelly, a stark contrast to the delicate image of cleansing smoke and spiritual healing.

They all laughed, shaking their heads at the absurdity of such a scene.

Then, it was back to business.

"Hey, boss, look." Hector nodded toward Ember, now back at the display, staring at the photo of her mother at the Red Cross gala.

Susan followed his gaze, then stepped forward. "I'll take it from here."

She crossed the room with practiced ease, positioning herself just close enough to be seen as an ally, close enough to interrupt whatever Ember might be starting to remember. "Your mother was so smart and so beautiful," Susan said, letting the words drift into the space between them.

Ember's eyes stayed on the picture. "She was beautiful, yes. And sometimes... she felt like a mystery. I don't know if I ever really knew her."

"She was your mother, Ember. Before you came along, she had her own stories, her own secrets. We never know our parents fully—it's more of a feeling than a knowing. You get what I mean?"

Ember just pointed at the photo. "Do you see this? It looks like her heart is glowing. At first, I thought it must be a camera flash. But there's nothing here it could be reflecting off."

"Probably someone's glasses. At our age, half the room has readers dangling from their pockets," Susan said, trying to lighten the mood.

The sun slipped lower, washing the garden in soft oranges and purples as twilight settled. The air shifted, leaves rustling in the cooling breeze as the crowd thinned out.

A faint clinking sound came up from behind.

"Ah, Hi NP. Headed out?" Susan's voice was steady as Dunn approached.

"Yes, it's time." Dunn offered a polite smile. "Ember, again, my deepest condolences." Hector, never far from his side, gave a curt nod before they turned and walked off.

Susan watched as Ember's eyes tracked Dunn through the thinning crowd; her focus sharp, unblinking. Dunn's gold bracelet flashed in the last of the light. Ember's lips pressed tight.

Susan stepped in close, resting a hand on her shoulder. "Stay on his good side, Ember," she said quietly.

Ember turned to her, squinting a little—uncertain, maybe even wary. Susan couldn't tell which version of herself Ember was seeing.

As the last rays of light faded, Ember turned away and let out a slow breath. "I will."

Susan gave a small nod, then stepped back. She told herself it was good advice. Necessary. But the ease with which she'd said it left a bitter taste.

CHAPTER 10

FOCUS

Ember opened her emails on her phone; one last check before walking to work.

"You've got to be kidding me," Ember remarked as her thumb landed on a message from Joy.

Subject: Sound Bath This Weekend

Yogis – Excited to share that we will have a guest teacher this weekend for a special workshop that incorporates sound bathing. And no, you don't have to wear your bathing suits! This is an opportunity to align your physical being with the frequencies of the universe. Get ready for a profound experience followed by the best sleep of your life.

See you soon!

Joy

How did I not see this for what it is before? Ember marveled. I signed up for a yoga instructor training, not a flipping séance. Is this cult recruitment? This is ridiculous. Too far.

Re: Sound Bath This Weekend

Hi Joy, Thanks for the update. A sound bath sounds like a nice way to float through the weekend. I'll be tied up with work so can't make it to training; perhaps my inner lawyer will show up for a cleansing.

Thanks,

Ember

Ember hit send and headed out. Now everything feels right in the universe. Susan's got it right, life is short. I must make it as fast as I can.

"The light in me bows to the light in you," Ember mocked aloud to herself. "Yeah, right. I cannot believe that I went to law school and was literally taught how to depose people and find the truth and yet, there I was, buying into a load of mystical drivel. What is wrong with me? Am I seriously that desperate? I'm such an idiot." She covered her face, shook away the thought, and emerged into a confident stride as she walked through the streets of Boston on her way to work.

"Suck it up, Ember." She continued aloud with her pep talk. "Get it together. These yogi truth-seekers with all of their namastes and savasanas and all that ommming are just a ridiculous way to ignore the truth and dodge reality. How about some see-ya-laters? Hmmm, Joy? How about those?"

"What are you looking at?" Ember snapped, her gaze narrowing at the young hipster in a mustard yellow sports jacket seated on a nearby bench. His eyes went wide for a moment before he quickly turned away, pretending to scroll through his phone, as Ember stormed by.

She put her headphones in and started her hard rock playlist; she needed someone to be angry with. She was about to break, so she screamed in her head along with the lyrics. "*No more lies, get out of my head!*" She pulsed in rhythm to the music as she approached the office building, the negative energy coursing through her body, providing release, and the anger delivering renewed conviction.

She walked into the office and there it was, rolled up neatly in the corner. Her damn yoga mat. How could she have let her partners see this here? "Oh no you don't, you're coming with me," she seethed. Ember snatched her yoga mat and hurried to the stairwell, running up the cement steps to the rooftop.

With the music as a soundtrack to her life, she stood with her feet apart and chest jutting out, yoga mat in arms, and surveyed the scene—like a superhero about to make their big move. "*One more breath and I come undone,*" the music shouted, and she internalized.

She dropped the mat into her hands, palms up like a serving platter, and then stepped with purpose, each footfall firm and measured, as she walked towards the edge of the building. The Atlantic Ocean, deep blue and frothy, undulated below. The music crescendoed, "*Can't hold this fury in!*" And with that, Ember closed her eyes and screamed from her heart. She whipped her mat around to hold it above her head and hurled it into the ocean.

She watched as it bobbed and unfurled, and wiped her hands clean of it.

"Back to work, work, and work some more," she sang in a jingle. And work she did.

CHAPTER 11

THAT NAGGING FEELING

Lawyers and law firms were not known for being warm and welcoming. Ember had known that coming into the profession, and she liked it that way—she wasn't drawn to emotional conversations or HR team-building games, either. Still, she had thought there would be more life within the walls of the firm.

Everything was a transaction—the relationships, the conversations, the work. Some people found comfort in it, preferring a world run by checklists and amusing themselves by snarking at typos. Perhaps she was being too harsh. The firm's people had wit. After pedigree, lawyers judged each other on the cleverness of their wit and banter.

Maybe she could fall into it and learn to love it. Was she being ungrateful? Could she justify feeling this internal conflict when her life was objectively privileged? And was it privileged if she dreaded it? She didn't know.

Her thoughts drifted, questioning and processing her life, and she let them. Why wouldn't she? It seemed a productive use of time as she sat chained to her desk at 11 p.m.

Rachel, a partner and Ember's assigned firm mentor, had a deal closing. Rachel instructed Ember to be on standby "just in case." Ember suspected that Rachel simply didn't want to be the only one in the office—it was too grim to be there alone at forty years old, surrounded by empty offices, with no underlings to comfort the ego. So, Ember sat and waited for the email that would announce the deal's closure and her release.

The email never came.

Ember awoke with a start, hearing someone's voice echoing down the hall. She was curled beneath her desk, her strategic hideout to avoid being seen if someone peeked in. Clutching her phone tightly against her chest, in case it buzzed, she uncurled and raised it to check her inbox. The bright light stung her eyes before they adjusted. No emergencies.

She pushed her chair back and emerged out of the cave into the golden light filtering in. She heard her office neighbor crack a can, burp, and then leave his office.

Gross. What a lovely way to start the day. How is that everyone can hear everything, but no one thinks people can hear them? Or maybe he just doesn't care.

She packed her purse, ready to head out, just long enough for a shower before returning.

As she walked down the hallway, Ember heard the clacking of a keyboard. She slowed, peering into an office as she passed. Inside sat a woman with a soft silhouette, outlined by the cold blue glow of a computer screen. The blinds were shut, and the woman was hunched forward, her head cocked to one side, chin tucked and jaw slack. Oily strands of hair framed her face, her eyes fixed on the screen, unblinking, as if she and the machine were one. Her face was vacant, expressionless. Flat.

This was focus. This was producing. Ember paused, tempted to take it in longer, but didn't want to get caught.

Was this what success looked like?

Was this Ember's future?

Her heart quickened. She forced the thought away and continued down the interior hallway with its drab, gray carpeted walls. She imagined herself ping-ponging off the walls, from one arm to another, trying to stay upright as she gasped for air.

Or was that what was actually happening?

The texture of the air suddenly smelled of mothballs. She was desperate for the freedom of the outside, jabbing the elevator button with the urgency of someone loosening a too-tight necktie.

Outside, she doubled over, hands on her knees for support, and drew in a deep breath before exhaling sharply, as if trying to expel everything suffocating inside her. Noticing people passing by noticing her, Ember collected herself and walked home.

Ember sank into her beige fabric couch, its cushions soft and slightly worn from years of late-night study sessions. Large windows framed her small city apartment, allowing streams of warm sunlight to fill the space. The warmth contrasted with the weight in her chest as she wrapped her fluffy robe around herself, feeling both comforted and confined. Steam from her shower lingered as she grabbed her phone and called Brendan, craving a connection with someone who perhaps understood.

"Hey, Ember! What's up?" Brendan's voice came through, bright and casual. He's always been there for her, especially since her parents died.

"Not much. Just trying to process everything that's been happening. Can I vent for a minute?" Ember asked, settling deeper into the couch.

"Of course. What's on your mind?"

Ember hesitated, gathering her thoughts. "It's like... I've been feeling this lingering heaviness. It's hard to explain, but it feels like my light is dimming." Her free hand instinctively covered her heart. "You know?"

"Yeah," Brendan replied, his tone shifting to one of concern. "It's not a sudden thing, is it? More like a slow fade?"

"Exactly," she said, relief washing over her. She wasn't crazy. "It's like a weight that keeps pressing down on me, making me feel like I'm disappearing."

Brendan sighed. "I get that. It's like your heart sinks into your stomach, and you're filled with dread. You start to resign yourself to everything around you."

"Yes! It's so suffocating. It feels like I'm a caged animal, trapped in a life I can't escape."

"You're not alone in that," Brendan said. "I've been there, too. It can feel like you're just going through the motions, turning off your insides to survive."

Ember's voice was barely a whisper. "It's exhausting."

"But remember," Brendan said, his tone firm yet comforting, "it's okay to feel this way. It doesn't mean you're weak; it means you're human. Humans are supposed to feel something. Our world requires that we feel nothing. We just have to find a way to do both, I guess."

As they continued to talk, Ember felt a flicker of hope. Maybe there was a way to reignite the light she thought she'd lost, even if it felt so distant right now.

CHAPTER 12

KEEP IT TOGETHER

Her hope was short lived. Such positive feelings lasted for shorter and shorter intervals. Hope and down. Hope and down. She had lost the ability to be buoyed by positive thinking.

Back at her desk, Ember stared at her computer screen, unmoving. She still wasn't used to the silence of a law firm, where the only sounds came from distant keyboards and printers. There were often days on end that she wouldn't see another soul.

Ember gripped the edge of her desk, her hands trembling as she fought the urge to break the silence.

How much fun would it be to just scream and see what happened?

She caught her reflection in the mirror on the back of her door, her made-to-look natural makeup and tight French bun—lawyer chic. Yet it all felt futile in the absence of anyone to see it. She was starting to feel a bit unhinged, desperate to keep her mask in place, to appear composed and professional even as her mind raced.

Keep it together, Ember. Keep it together. The mantra echoed in her thoughts, her daily lifeline that felt more like a desperate plea today.

A notification appeared on her screen, a new email.

Subject: Come to my office.

I have an assignment for you.

Thx.

Rachel

Her pulse quickened as she fought against the encroaching sense of dread.

Turn your insides off. Go through the motions. Ember reached for a pen and a notepad, pushed away from her desk, and checked the mirror. She smoothed a flyaway hair and brushed out the wrinkles in her navy-blue pants.

With one last look at her quiet office—which moments ago felt suffocating but now seemed like an oasis—she headed toward Rachel's office, steeling herself to smile.

Ember sat across from Rachel, papers scattered between them on her partner-level executive desk. This was one of the perks of being a partner—the privilege of choosing one of three styles of big-boy desks.

That's what I'm working for? Ember thought at the sight of it. One of three styles of big-boy desks. Great. Thanks, boss! Pathetic.

Ember could sense tension in the air but couldn't see what was on Rachel's screen. Her expression changed, her face paling as she whispered, "Oh God."

"What is it?"

Rachel looked up; her eyes concerned. "It's Jon. He just had a heart attack. He's in the hospital."

Ember felt the blood drain from her face. Jon? The Big Cat partner. "What? Is he okay?"

"I don't know. They're still assessing, but said it's serious," Rachel replied, her voice shaking.

Ember sat back, stunned. "This doesn't make any sense. I just saw him the other day and he seemed great."

"You know, when I joined this firm, I thought I was doing the right thing for my career and my family. I had a good job at Reebok before I went to law school." Rachel's upper lip quivered. "I thought I was bored at Reebok, but now I see that might have been okay."

Ember sensed that this heavy news was prompting Rachel to reflect on her own choices. "What do you mean?"

"I missed my son's first day of Kindergarten last week because of work," she admitted, tears pricking her eyes.

Ember felt a pang of empathy. "What's his name?"

"Max," Rachel replied, glancing at a picture on her desk.

Rachel took a deep breath and continued, "First, we had David with his divorce, then Ted with clinical burnout, and now Sarah's complications are keeping her on bedrest during her pregnancy. And don't even get me started on Janice and her malpractice suit over substance abuse. It feels like this place is falling apart."

Ember nodded, absorbing the gravity of Rachel's words.

Rachel straightened her shoulders, realizing that she had unloaded too much to an associate, and to one whose parents just died. She shifted into a more professional tone. "We need Jon, so we'll have to wait. The deal has a false deadline anyway. Opposing counsel is just trying to rush us because of their vacation."

"Well, this is just how it is sometimes." And with that, Rachel stood and walked by Ember and out of the office, leaving Ember alone.

Ember stared at the scattered papers on the desk, her pen hovering uselessly over her notepad. Rachel's chair sat empty, spinning slightly from her abrupt exit. The office felt unnaturally quiet, the distant hum of voices and keyboards muffled as if the air had thickened.

Her gaze drifted to the picture of Max on Rachel's desk—a grinning boy caught mid-laugh, a dog's tongue slobbering against his cheek. Rachel's words lingered in the silence. Missed milestones, crumbling colleagues, Jon's heart attack. The relentless weight of it all pressed down like a storm cloud, heavy and unresolved.

Ember shifted in her seat, her pen finally dropping onto the desk with a clatter. She glanced toward the door. Empty. No sign of Rachel. No instructions. No clarity. Just the papers between them and a lingering question: Now what?

CHAPTER 13

THE SHE-SHED

Ember didn't go home. Instead, she drove to her parents' house, the one now under her name. She hadn't decided what to do with it yet, but today, she felt pulled there. It sat at the edge of town, an olive house with white shutters and a stone walkway, surrounded by woods that offered a type of privacy not typically found in the area.

She parked and approached the door, key in hand, but couldn't bring herself to go inside. Even from the doorstep, she could smell wood polish and faint lavender, a reminder of her mother's habits.

Ember inhaled, "Mom," she smiled at the feeling. She was desperate to hug her, to feel near her.

She went around to the backyard and there it was—her mother's she-shed. Ember hadn't been inside in years. The grass crunched under her shoes as she approached the shed. This had been her mother's haven, tucked away from everything.

The shed sat at the forest's edge, its log cabin exterior blending into the landscape. Large glass windows faced the woods, framed by weathered wooden beams. Ivy curled around the corners, embracing the shed as part of the forest.

She opened the door, and the familiar scent of sawdust and incense hit her. Inside, her mother lingered—a forgotten coffee mug, a stack of notebooks, framed photos and piles of old photos that never made it into albums.

Ember moved to the desk and picked up a handful of photos. She flipped through them absently: hiking trips from decades ago, sunburned faces, her mother's easy smile, her father's arm slung loosely around her shoulders. Then, the images shifted. The more recent photos were different: stiff poses at corporate events, champagne glasses raised, those toothy smiles that looked practiced.

"Work, work, work," Ember whispered, a phrase her mother used to say when lost in thought.

One photo stopped her cold.

NP Dunn, in a charcoal blue suit, hand clasped around her mother's arm. Not in a casual way, but firm, possessive. Ember recognized that grip. He'd done the same to her at the Celebration of Life.

She flipped through more photos, faster now. Dunn was everywhere. Standing just behind her father, speaking at a podium while James and Cynthia sat on the stage beside him, their expressions strained. In candid shots, only Dunn seemed aware of the camera—alert, composed, in control. Her parents looked…diminished. Like the light had slowly drained from them, frame by frame.

Memories rushed back, now seen in a different light—her parents' hushed arguments, talks about family trips and escapes that never happened, her father's increasingly distant eyes, and those rare moments of genuine joy, like Van Morrison.

Dunn wasn't a friend; he'd had leverage.

Ember's stomach dropped.

How?

He must've had something on them. A secret? A threat? Or maybe it was more insidious—*dependence*. He helped them scale. And once they were too deep in, too entangled in the success he engineered, he made sure they couldn't walk away.

"Stay on his good side, Ember." Susan's words rang in her ears. She hadn't been mentoring her; she'd been warning her!

It hit her like a punch: It was Dunn who kept them working late. Who pushed every expansion, every deal. Who benefited most from their exhaustion. Who built the machine they couldn't escape.

Ember's throat tightened.

It wasn't a single thing. It was the sum of things. The environment. The pressure. All of it leading to this moment.

Her parents weren't just absent. They were taken from her, one sacrifice at a time. And now they were gone.

For what?

Anger swelled inside her, rising through her shoulders. Then the heat and sweat of rage.

"It was all for nothing!" Ember cried, sweeping her arms across the desk. The mug and frames shattered, shards of porcelain and glass scattering across the floor. Her breath quickened as the walls of the shed closed in.

She burst outside, running into the woods, dodging branches and rocks. When she couldn't go further, she stopped and doubled over, hands on her knees, gasping for air. Her vision blurred, she looked up to the sky and she screamed into the trees, raw and hoarse.

And then it was done.

The sound faded, leaving silence. When her breathing slowed, Ember straightened and looked around. She used to play in these woods; Enchanted, she'd called them. A clearing she'd never seen before caught her eye.

"What the?" She felt pulled towards it.

In the center of the clearing lay an emerald green yoga mat. It seemed out of place, yet familiar. Her heart tightened. *Mom?*

She approached, her steps slow, cautious. She was scared of what this space might hold, or perhaps that it held nothing. The urge to feel close to her mother pulled her forward. She knelt, pressing her hands to the places where her mother's hands had once rested. She stretched her arms out long and brought her hips back to rest her head on the mat, her forehead touching where her mother's had once touched. She pressed her hands firmly into the mat and lifted her hips up into downward facing dog, an inverted V-shape that offers a different perspective, a chance to see the world upside down. She walked her feet forward, and placed them at the top of the mat, rising to stand tall. Her hands down by her sides, palms lifted to the sky, open.

Suddenly, a deep hum filled the air, and the ground shifted. The forest twinkled and a white light swirled into a vortex beneath her. Before she could move, the clearing spun with a force that pulled her downward.

"Where are we going?" she thought as the world turned dark.

Thud, she landed.

The first thing that she noticed is that the air felt different. Ember blinked and looked around. This wasn't her parents' yard. It wasn't the woods.

It was somewhere else entirely.

CHAPTER 14

A CLEARING
IN THE WOODS

E mber's hands instinctively pressed into the cool, damp rock beneath her. She knelt, taking in the raw, earthen scent, an aroma both ancient and alive. Her fingers traced the textures of the stone, feeling its solidness, grounding herself in this unexpected world.

"Hello?" she called, her voice echoing, almost swallowed by the vastness. The only response was the soft drip of water somewhere deeper within.

She rose slowly, her muscles tense. She adjusted to the dim, burnt orange light that filled the cave. It seemed to pulse, a faint glow that barely revealed her surroundings yet was enough to hint at what lay ahead. There was no exit in sight.

"The only way out is through," she said to herself, drawing a steadying breath. With one last look around, she moved forward, her footsteps muffled against the stone floor.

As she ventured deeper, a low, rhythmic drumbeat began to thrum around her, subtle at first but then intensifying until it

seeped into her bones. The vibration settled in her core, resonating through her waist, her hips, down to her legs. It was
primal, raw—unlike anything she'd felt before.

Without thought, Ember's body responded. She dropped
into a crouch, knees bent, her torso swaying with the rhythm.
Her hands found their way to her legs, steadying herself as
she gave in to the beat's call. The sway became a lunge, then a
twist, her hands reaching, scooping the air in front of her as if
clearing a path through invisible resistance. Her movements
grew more fluid, graceful, with power rising within her.

Then, her arms stretched wide, one reaching high as though
parting the very air, opening a curtain to whatever lay beyond.
She softened into the movement. It started to come from within.
Instinctual, and free. She felt wild, untamed, and for the first
time, she understood the full, unrestrained strength within her.

The shadows on the flame-licked walls of the cave danced
with her, a mirror of her soul's expression. She was both the
dancer and the dance, a force boundless and unyielding. This
was her space. Her moment. Her ecstasy. She was dancing
with the universe.

And then—she felt it. A presence, unseen but unmistakable. Her movements didn't falter; instead, she embraced the
awareness. It felt strong, familiar yet mysterious, a part of the
cave yet somehow separate. She turned her attention toward
it. Her gaze was steady, her body still swaying, low and wide,
like the drumbeat had rooted her to the earth.

The presence didn't feel threatening. It pulsed with energy
that resonated with hers, encouraging her, amplifying her

wildness. Her heart swelled, welcoming whatever it was. Why are you here? What are you? Her mind wondered, yet her soul seemed to already understand.

The beat surged, growing louder, deeper, and Ember suddenly noticed she was barefoot. The earth beneath her feet felt alive, grounding her and feeding her energy back to her. As the rhythm crescendoed, she surrendered entirely, her body moving on its own accord—jumping, pulsing, beaming, and electric, a conduit for the universe's boundless energy.

A surge of light burst from her heart, blindingly bright, illuminating the cave in a flash that reached every crevice. She felt the connection to everything—every stone, every shadow, every pulse of the drumbeat.

And then, just as suddenly as it began, the moment subsided. The beat faded, leaving her breathless, heart pounding, eyes wide open in the abrupt quiet.

Ember glanced around, reorienting herself. And there, leaning casually against the wall, was a man. His gaze met hers.

"I love your energy," he said, his voice warm. He was tall and lean, his brown hair pulled back in a casual manbun, with trim, close-cropped facial hair. His clothes, a simple gray tank top with black cotton joggers, seemed to blend with the earth around them, as though he belonged to this place.

Ember smiled. She felt her energy settle, while still humming beneath her skin. Bowing her head in appreciation, she acknowledged his presence. Somehow, she knew they had a shared understanding that this moment, this place, had awakened something within her.

Ember looked up, curious. "Who are you?"

He uncrossed his arms and extended a hand. "Derek. And you?"

"Ember. How'd you find me?"

"I was out for a walk and saw light coming from inside the cave. Usually, when you're in a cave, you're looking for the light to get out. But this light was coming from within." He beamed. "I had to check it out—and there you were."

Ember nodded, glancing around the cave before meeting his eyes again. "Where am I?"

Derek snapped his fingers, like locking in an idea. "Let me show you," he said, gesturing toward the entrance with an easy confidence.

She walked beside him, each step making the energy inside her settle into a warm, steady pulse. The air shifted as they exited the cave—cool and fresh, laced with the scent of pine.

They reached the forest edge, and Ember paused, pushing aside a low-hanging branch to see what lay beyond. She gasped.

Just down the hill stretched a vibrant gathering—a festival set in a valley beneath snow-capped mountains, with a river winding through the landscape. Rows of colorful tents covered the field. The air was alive with the scent of food, the sound of music, and the warmth of sunlight.

Ember and Derek walked down into the festival. The scene was mesmerizing. People were scattered throughout the valley, some on yoga mats in flowing, meditative poses, others seated at easels, their brushes moving over canvases. Here and there, groups of friends relaxed on blankets, sipping out of coconuts.

Ember noticed a woman in a metallic skirt, a gold bandeau top, and fluffy boots, her purple-streaked hair catching the light as she twirled a neon hoop in graceful circles.

"Hungry?" Derek asked, nodding toward a table stacked with bright fruits and muffins.

She shook her head, still taking it all in. She felt at peace, as if she'd found a place she hadn't known she was searching for.

"This is Resonance," Derek said. "We call ourselves the Breathers."

"The Breathers?" Ember asked.

"We live in both worlds," he explained. "We move among those who've forgotten themselves in the everyday world. But we also come here. For some, all it takes to enter Resonance is to close their eyes and breathe."

Ember thought back to her mother's yoga mat and the doorway it had opened. She felt a growing understanding.

"How long have you been here?" she asked.

"Time is different here," he said, shrugging. "What feels like a week in Resonance might be five minutes in the real world. It's like the best, most refreshing vacation you've ever had."

A bark broke through their conversation. A brown hound, draped in a colorful scarf, trotted toward them with a friendly tail wag.

"Frank!" Derek grinned and greeted his dog. Frank sniffed Ember, gave an approving nudge, then returned to Derek's side.

"Come on," Derek said, leading her toward a large, inviting tent nearby. Inside, people sat on low cushions in rich colors— blue, crimson, gold, violet—engaged in relaxed conversations and sipping tea. The air carried a warm, subtle fragrance of herbs.

At the center of the tent sat a woman with dark hair flowing in loose waves around her shoulders. Her robe-dress, a rich shade of green adorned with delicate vine-like patterns, seemed to match the natural ease of her presence. She moved with purpose, selecting herbs and combining them with practiced care.

"Ember, this is Jade," Derek said.

Jade looked up, offering a warm smile. "Welcome, Ember," she said, her voice gentle. She held out a cup of tea. "A blend of chamomile, lavender, and a hint of fresh mint, with notes of sage and lemon balm." The aroma was floral and fresh.

"Would you like some?" Jade asked.

"Thank you," Ember accepted the cup and sipped a brew that both relaxed her body and sharpened her senses.

As Ember settled onto the cushions beside Derek and Jade, she wondered if she had finally arrived somewhere designed for her, or if it was all just too perfect. She sipped the tea, willing herself to relax, even as part of her stayed alert, ready to run if she had to.

CHAPTER 15

FACES OF RESONANCE

Ember took a moment to absorb her surroundings and notice the warmth of the cup in her hands, and then turned back to her new friends.

"So, what do you all do outside of… this?" Ember asked, gesturing at the scene around them.

Jade gave a small smile. "I work with brains, let's just say. I used to be a neurosurgeon, but things changed, and I realized there was more to healing than just the physical."

Ember raised her eyebrows. "That's… not exactly light work."

Jade nodded. "And you?"

"I'm an associate at a big law firm," Ember replied, feeling the weight of her usual title. "Mostly loan documents. Corporate stuff."

Derek chuckled. "Sounds intense. I'm in product development at a tech company. Lots of late nights and deadlines." He leaned back, giving Ember an amused look. "It's nothing like this place, but there's something satisfying about building things from scratch."

"Hmmm, yes." Ember pretended to understand. "So, how did you end up here?"

Derek shrugged, looking thoughtful. "Honestly, I stumbled into it. Sometimes, the right place just finds you."

"Ugh, Derek, you're always so vague," Jade chided.

They all paused as Frank, Derek's dog, wandered over and settled at his feet, giving a long, exaggerated yawn.

"What's Frank's deal?" Ember asked with a giggle.

"Oh, he's a Vizsla." Derek said.

Ember shook her head. "No, I mean—how did he end up here?"

Derek reached down and scratched behind Frank's ears. "Ah. Well… Frank's not your average dog. Sometimes I think he's more tuned in than half the people I know. Honestly, it feels like he understands this place better than I do."

Jade laughed, nodding. "It's true. Frank's got his own wisdom."

Ember couldn't help but laugh, too. "A 'woke' dog in Resonance. Makes sense, I guess."

Just then, a familiar voice called her name. "Ember."

She turned, her heart skipping as she recognized the figure approaching. "Joy?"

Joy nodded, her face calm yet curious. "I knew you'd find your way here."

Ember's cheeks flushed. "I… I owe you an apology. I know I was a bit dismissive about that sound bath you recommended. I've just had a lot going on."

Joy's expression softened. "It's fine, Ember. We all get caught up in life."

"Jade, Derek—this is Joy, she was my yoga instructor training teacher…" Ember trailed off.

"Oh, we know Joy," they said in unison.

"How did you get here?" Joy directed to Ember.

"Well, I stepped onto my mom's old yoga mat. It was out in the forest behind the house… and then there was this vortex. Next thing I knew, I was dropped into a cave, and that's where Derek found me. Just now."

Joy studied her for a moment, nodding. "Interesting."

Jade leaned in, her tone respectful. "Joy's been coming to Resonance a long time. She knows this place better than most of us."

Joy met Ember's gaze. "You're ready to know more, aren't you?"

Ember took a steadying breath. "Yes. I'm ready."

Jade rose and gestured toward the teapot. "I'll get us some more tea. We might be here for a while."

Once everyone was settled again, Joy began her story, her voice rhythmic, recounting a tale as old as Resonance itself. "In the beginning, Resonance was untouched—a realm of pure light and creation, held together by the Prism, a source of energy as natural as a star. It radiated light, feeding the souls of those who ventured here, grounding them in purpose and clarity."

Ember leaned forward, captivated.

"But then, someone who had lost his virtue found Resonance. A man you know. NP Dunn." Joy said.

"What? He's here?" Ember asked.

"Let her go on," Jade cut in. "I've never heard the story in full, just bits and pieces."

Ember quieted, as Joy continued.

"Yes, he's here. He began his life's journey creating surveillance systems and other advanced technologies to aid in disaster relief with good intentions, working alongside people who shared his vision, like your parents. They believed in what they were doing, saw it as a way to help humanity. But as Dunn's ambitions grew, he started crossing ethical lines, driven by the pressure to deliver bigger results."

Joy's voice grew darker. "Dunn discovered Resonance and saw the Prism for what it was—a source of unlimited light and influence. He realized that if he could control the light here, he could control the people who accessed it. He saw the inhabitants of Resonance as obstacles, those who questioned and resisted compliance. By suppressing their light, he could dull their awareness and influence them back in the world you just came from, what most refer to simply—though perhaps not accurately—as the real world."

Ember's grip on her teacup tightened, her mind racing with implications. "The worlds are linked?" Ember asked.

"Right," Derek nodded. "If Dunn puts out your light here in Resonance, it cuts you off from who you really are in the real world. Without that core part of you—your virtue—you lose direction and end up following anyone who takes charge. That's how Dunn pulls people under his control."

"Take away their light, and they cannot see, they will follow blindly," Joy continued, her expression somber. "That became his goal; his motto."

"But I just got here, so that means not everyone from the real world is in Resonance." Ember said. "Why doesn't Dunn just target people who don't know about this place and don't care, and leave the Breathers—people like you who do know—alone?"

"And now people like you, Ember. You're a Breather," Jade corrected. "You've arrived." She paused. "Like you, Ember, people find their way here at different points. Dunn can't always predict which hires might end up becoming Breathers. All sorts of things can open someone's eyes—a loss, a birth, a powerful experience, or just a simple walk in the park. Once someone becomes a Breather, they're a risk to his whole system. They start to question things, and that can spread. Dunn doesn't want to take that chance."

"Okay, so we get here through awareness and seeking truth. Dunn might have awareness, but not the truth of heart. So, how does he get here?" Ember asked.

"Dunn's clever, I'll give him that," Joy admitted. "He figured out a way to enter Resonance by putting himself in life-threatening situations. That pure, desperate will to live is what opens the door for him."

"Every time?" Ember asked, wide-eyed.

"Every time," Joy nodded. "And once he got here, he brought his drones, his loyal followers—anyone willing to push his agenda. We call them the Watchmen."

"That's one thing I've never understood," Jade began. "How did Dunn get his Watchmen and technology here? It must be hard enough for him to come and go."

"Now that, I don't know." Joy shrugged.

Ember whispered, "And the Prism...?"

Joy let out a heavy sigh. "It still lives up on the mountain top as a beacon of this realm, but he's covered it with a material that absorbs light instead of reflecting it. So, when people come to Resonance for the first time, their light is taken upon arrival—pulled into the Prism and trapped there. For those of us who were already here, we're still connected to the Prism, but now it's like a one-way drain. Our light keeps getting drawn into it, but it can't give anything back. Our lights grow dimmer, weaker, and I imagine even the Prism's light and power is fading."

Ember thought back to her experience in Joy's yoga training class – that cave, her light. She had been here. The danger: she had felt it chill through her body.

"You can see why I was so curious to meet you in that cave, Ember," Derek said. "You weren't just holding onto your light— you were amplifying it, radiating it, even dancing with it. You're the first person to enter and be free of Dunn's twisted hold."

Ember's face tightened with anger. "Well then that shows it's possible to stop him. Why hasn't anyone?"

Joy's expression was grave. "Others have tried. They journeyed up the mountain to confront him, but no one who has gone up has come down. They're stuck up there below the summit in loops of forgetting, bombarded by distractions and mental chaos. We call them the Wanderers. His drones spread confusion and doubt. These Wanderers meander aimlessly. They don't even know what they're searching for anymore."

Ember swallowed, Joy's words settling deep in her chest. She shivered, picturing the Wanderers, caught in endless loops, stripped of purpose. She imagined herself up there: lost, forgotten.

The thought should have terrified her.

But she didn't feel fear.

She felt fury.

CHAPTER 16

SONDER

Jade sat cross-legged, her earrings catching the fading light. "So, picture this—I'm leading a meditation class, everything perfectly aligned. Everyone's breathing in sync, and I'm in the zone, thinking, *This is peak mindfulness*." She raised her hands as if framing a masterpiece. "And then—thud!—a cat jumps onto my mat."

Ember leaned forward. "Where did it come from?"

Jade threw up her hands. "How am I supposed to know? I had my eyes closed!"

"So, what did you do?" Joy chuckled, her arms wrapped around her knees.

"What could I do?" Jade shrugged. "I kept going! I'm guiding everyone through this calm, reflective state, and meanwhile, this cat is staring at me like I interrupted its practice. Then it sprawled out on my mat and started purring. After class, someone actually asked, 'Was the cat part of the meditation? To test our focus?' Like I planned it!"

"Did it stay the whole time?" Ember asked.

"Oh, it stayed," Jade said. "The whole session."

Joy tilted her head, a knowing smile spreading across her face. "That's a cat for you. They ignore you when you want their attention and show up the moment you don't."

The group laughed, the sound light and easy, flowing into the stillness of the evening. Even Frank gave a soft woof, his tail thumping against the ground.

As the laughter faded, Joy rubbed her arms and shivered. "Is it just me, or did it get chilly?"

Derek stood, brushing off his hands. "I'll get a fire going. It won't take long."

He moved easily, gathering dry branches and stacking them neatly in a small clearing. With a quick strike of flint, the first spark came to life, growing into a crackling fire. He gestured for the group to join him and sat down. The fire highlighted his sharp features as the others gathered around.

Ember sat cross-legged. The murmur of the festival faded into the background as she took a deep breath, gathering her thoughts. She exhaled.

"My parents just died," she said, her voice steady. "Car accident."

Jade's expression softened. "I'm so sorry, Ember."

Joy reached out, resting a hand on Ember's shoulder. "That's a lot to carry."

Ember nodded, her gaze fixed on the ground. "Thanks. It's awful. And what makes me feel even more awful is that it's left me thinking... If I could just be successful faster, maybe I'd have the power to enjoy my life. You know? Before it's too late."

Across from her, Derek let out a short, dry laugh.

Joy and Jade both turned to him, glaring. Jade whacked his arm, a signal to behave.

"Sorry," he said, raising his hands defensively. "I don't mean to be insensitive. It's just... that's how it works. The systems are designed for you to run out of time."

Ember's gaze lifted to meet his, defiance in her eyes. "Then don't you think it's time for something more morally sound?"

Before anyone could answer, a warm, radiant glow began to emanate from Ember's chest. It started faint, just a flicker. Ember clutched her chest instinctively.

"What's happening?"

Frank sat upright, his intelligent eyes watching her as if understanding the significance of the moment.

Joy placed a hand over her heart. "It's your light," she said. "Your soul. Your true self. The part of you that remembers what matters."

The glow pulsed outward and then expanded into a brilliant white light that bathed the entire group. Ember's heart pulsated with an electric energy. It was as if the very essence of her soul had awakened and was now reaching out and intertwining with the energy of the world around her. The others watched, captivated. "Why is it doing this?" Ember asked, eyes wide, hand still over her chest.

Joy's voice softened. "When you asked if it's time for something more morally sound... that might have been the moment it started. You weren't just speaking for yourself. You were speaking for all of us. You saw the system for what it is and said:

we deserve better." She nodded toward the glow surrounding them. "That's not just light… that's Sonder."

"Sonder?" Ember asked.

"It's what happens when your light—your soul, your truth—reaches beyond just you," Joy said. "When it hits you that everyone around you is living a life as vivid and complex as yours. That they're the main character in their story, just like you are in yours."

"Think of it like this," Jade said, leaning in. "Light is your candle. Sonder isn't lighting someone else's—it's realizing they have one, too. But if two people really see each other like that? If those lights come together? That's the kind of fire that spreads. That gets noticed." She glanced up toward the mountain. "Maybe even by the Prism."

Jade turned back to Ember. "When that kind of awareness spreads—when people begin to see each other clearly, and act on it—that's what threatens Dunn most. Because his power depends on isolation. Disconnection." Her expression hardened. "That's what makes you dangerous to him. He doesn't just steal light—he severs the link between Resonance and the real world. We found this place before his control took hold. That's why we can still come back and remember who we are."

Joy rested her hand on the ground between them. "But when we leave? It fades. What we learn here—what we feel—it slips away. Like waking from a dream. And little by little, that forgetfulness wears down your light."

Ember's voice dropped to a whisper. "So, people lose themselves… not here, necessarily, but when they go back."

Jade nodded, and then reached over and touched Ember's arm. "You have your light, Ember. You're here to help us. You're here to defeat Dunn."

Derek stood. "This might be our last chance to break the Watchmen's hold on Resonance. And Ember isn't going to end up a Wanderer if I have anything to do with it. I'll go with her."

"Go with me? Where?" Ember asked.

Frank barked once, a low, commanding sound that made it clear that he, too, was ready for the fight.

Joy placed a hand on Ember's shoulder, grounding her in the moment. "If you succeed, Ember, light will be restored to everyone in Resonance and they will remember their virtue. They will remember why they come to Resonance and what they learn. They will no longer feel the nagging emptiness, the inner conflict and sense that something is wrong but no way to pinpoint it."

Joy paused. "But you need to know—this threatens Dunn and his Watchmen's control. They'll stop at nothing to keep their power."

Ember's hands trembled as she processed the weight of her responsibility. "And if I fail?"

"You won't fail, because I'm coming too," Jade said, resolute. "You have your light, but we've found other tools to help us here."

"Let me show you," Derek said. He disappeared into the shadows, returning moments later with a long, crystalline sword. The blade shimmered in the firelight, its facets catching and refracting the light into a rainbow of colors. The weapon looked brutally dangerous—its jagged edges and sharp points better suited for bludgeoning than slicing, like a spiked club forged from raw crystal.

Derek held it out, turning it so the firelight danced along its surface. "My light's not what it used to be. But this?" He held up the sword. "This'll do just fine for now."

"Only one?" Ember asked. "If Dunn and the Watchmen are as powerful as you say they are, one-to-one combat isn't going to get us very far."

"Don't be fooled! It's not just a weapon—it's a source of energy and strength. It can break through the strongest barriers, even ones the Watchmen believe are impenetrable." He paused, palming the jagged surface. "I found it in a cave long ago. To most, it was just a dull piece of crystal, nothing more. But for me, it came alive. Somehow, it resonates with me—it holds power in my hands."

Jade's robes shifted as she reached for the locket around her neck. She opened it, revealing a small bundle of dried herbs inside, glowing with a neon green light. "My healing abilities may not be as strong as they once were. But, these herbs? They're more than they seem."

Ember looked at each of them in turn, her light still pulsing. "We're going to climb the Watchmen's Mountain," she said, her voice stronger now. "We're going to restore light to everyone."

Frank barked, as if protesting being left out. The group turned to him, and he wagged his tail and spun in a circle before flopping down in front of Derek. He nudged the crystal sword with his nose, then looked up with big eyes.

Derek laughed. "Alright, alright, Frank. You're coming too. We couldn't do this without you."

Frank wagged his tail harder, his tongue lolling as he rested his head on his paws.

Joy, however, stood, her hands on her hips. "I can't come with you," she said with regret. "The Breathers need me here. If you go, the Watchmen will fight back harder than ever. We need to keep the community strong, united. They'll need to understand what you're doing and why."

"Sunrise yoga tomorrow," Jade reminded Joy. "It's always been the time for clarity, for connection. It's the perfect space to explain."

Joy considered this for a moment before nodding. "Good idea. I'll tell them at the close of yoga tomorrow morning— you're all joining, by the way." She winked. "After that, you start your ascent, and we'll hold things down here."

The group sat in silence.

Then Ember broke the tension with a smile. "I've always liked impossible odds."

As the group stood, Ember looked at each of them—Derek with his crystal sword, Jade holding her locket, Frank wagging his tail, and Joy resolute. *I guess this is the crew.*

"We've got everything we need." Jade gestured with open palms to the group.

Frank barked once, as if sealing their pact.

As the group dispersed, Jade lingered. "Come on," Jade said as she looped her arm through Ember's. "You'll need your strength for tomorrow. I'll show you where you can rest."

"I don't know if I'll be able to sleep," Ember said.

Jade led her to a small cluster of tents tucked just beyond

the clearing. "You will. This place has a way of giving you what you need, even if you don't realize it yet."

They reached a modest but comfortable tent with soft woven mats and a bundle of blankets neatly stacked inside. Jade pulled back the flap and gestured for Ember to enter. "It's not much, but it's peaceful here. You'll be safe."

Ember stepped inside. "Thank you."

Jade nodded, her hand lingering on the edge of the tent flap. "Help yourself to whatever you need. There's water by the entrance, and those boots in the corner might be good for the trek tomorrow." She paused. "You've already done more than you know, Ember. Rest now. Tomorrow, we start something bigger than all of us."

With that, Jade let the flap fall back into place and walked away, leaving Ember in the stillness. Ember sank onto the mat, wrapping a blanket around her shoulders as she closed her eyes.

Change was coming.

CHAPTER 17

LET'S BEGIN AGAIN

The shuffle of footsteps woke Ember, mingling with the hum of voices and the chirping of morning birds. Groggy, she blinked as early light filtered through her tent.

She pushed the tent flap aside and peered out. Streams of people were walking towards the main clearing by the river. Vibrant yoga mats in every color draped over their shoulders like a moving rainbow. The mountains in the distance stood like silent guardians. Ember yawned, the crisp morning air filling her lungs.

Her gaze dropped to the ground beside her bed.

"What the?"

There, neatly rolled and propped against the tent wall, was her yoga mat—the same one she'd hurled into the ocean. She crouched down and touched it, half expecting it to vanish like a mirage. But it was solid. Real.

I guess "go with the flow" applies here, she thought, shaking off her disbelief.

Ember picked up the mat, gave it a quiet, half-joking apology, and slung it under her arm. Joining the stream of people, she

94

spotted Jade and Derek a short distance ahead and quickened her pace to catch up.

"Morning," Jade said. "Looks like you're ready."

Ember held up her mat, giving it a wry look. "Apparently!"

Frank barked just ahead of them as he pawed at something near a cluster of rocks. Derek tilted his head, curiosity lighting up his face as he approached and crouched beside the dog.

"What've you got there, buddy?" Derek said, nudging Frank aside to pick up a small, misshapen hunk of metal. He turned it over in his hands, "Hah! What is this, part of an old hinge? A piece of scrap?" His grin widened as he held it up. "Nice work, Treasurepup. Always finding the good stuff." Frank wagged his tail furiously and gave a proud little bark.

"Boys," Ember muttered, rolling her eyes. "You're acting like you've struck gold."

Derek straightened, slipping the object into his pocket with exaggerated reverence. "Hey, treasure is in the eye of the beholder," he said, winking. "Besides, Frank and I are building a museum of useless things." Ember shook her head but couldn't stop her smile. Their enthusiasm was ridiculous—and strangely comforting.

Derek grinned. "Front row?" He gestured toward the clearing ahead, where the mats were being arranged in neat rows, parallel to the river and facing the mountains beyond.

"Front row," Ember agreed.

They placed their mats side by side and settled into seated positions. Joy stepped onto a platform at the front of the crowd. Her flowing, colorful attire and short red waves complemented her deep, rich skin. She embodied the harmony of the setting. She surveyed the crowd, her hazel eyes warm, her smile serene.

"Look around you," Joy began, her voice steady. "This morning is a gift, and so is the breath in your lungs. What you do with it is up to you. Choose to show up. Choose to be fully alive."

The crowd stilled.

"Today, I'm here to remind you that being fully alive means more than simply existing. It means taking risks. It means stepping into the unknown and trusting that the strength you need will find you. Today, through breath and movement, we will remember what it feels like to be fully alive. Let's begin."

The group moved as one through the sunrise vinyasa sequence, their bodies bending and stretching as one. Ember felt the tension in her shoulders release with each inhale, and the fire of determination grow with every exhale.

As the flow came to an end, Joy guided them into Savasana, the final resting pose. Hundreds of people lay still on their mats, eyes closed, their chests rising and falling in quiet rhythm. The sun climbed higher, bathing the group in its warm, golden light.

Joy's voice carried over the stillness. "When you're ready, begin to wiggle your fingers and toes, returning movement to your body."

"Remember this moment. This stillness. The world will pull at you, challenge you, distract you—but here's the truth: You carry this strength, this breath, with you everywhere you go. Fully alive. That's your choice, every day."

The crowd stirred, stretching, turning onto their sides, and sitting up.

Joy's gaze swept over them. "Thank you for sharing this morning, this practice." She brought her palms together at her heart and bowed her head. "Namaste."

As the class began to stir, Joy raised her hands, calling for their attention.

"Before you roll up your mats and step back into your day, there's something important I need to share with you," she said.

The crowd quieted.

"This morning, we practiced stepping into our breath and courage. Now, a few among us will take that courage further—up the mountain." Joy pointed up to the peak of the Watchmen's Mountain behind her.

She paused.

"I've been waiting for the day I could once again end class with the words, 'The light in me bows to the light in you,' as they were always meant to be spoken. And today, I believe we are closer to that reality than ever."

The air in the clearing felt heavy with anticipation.

"Today is special," Joy continued, her voice resonating with purpose. "We gather not just to move and breathe, but to witness something extraordinary. Ember has joined us, carrying her light. Somehow, she escaped Dunn's grasp. That alone is nothing short of a miracle."

Murmurs rippled through the crowd, a mix of awe, disbelief, and unspoken questions—why her?

Joy held up a hand, her expression steady but kind, as if to quiet their doubts. "I know some of you are wondering, 'Why Ember?' And the truth is, I don't know. None of us do.

For reasons we can't fully understand, Ember carries the light. What I do know is this: it is here, and it is real. She is proof that our light can still exist, even in the face of all that we've lost."

Her voice softened. "This is not about why. It's about what. What Ember's light means for all of us. It means hope. It means possibility. It means that the fight for our humanity is not over."

The crowd sat motionless now, every gaze locked on Joy.

"Ember will begin her ascent today," Joy continued. "She will not go alone. Jade, Derek, and Frank will join her."

She gestured toward the front and called the four of them to step forward. They rose and joined Joy on the platform.

Joy placed a hand on Ember's shoulder and turned to address the group again. "If you see them today—before they leave—please, offer what you can. Your words, your wisdom, your strength. We all have something to give, and it matters."

The murmur of the crowd grew warm, with whispers of agreement rippling through them.

Ember felt the weight of their hope.

"We, the Breathers, will stay strong here," Joy said, her tone rising with conviction. "We are their foundation, their force. Let this morning's flow remind you—our power is in our connection."

Pressing her hands together at her heart, she bowed her head.

The group rose, one by one, bowing toward the front. "Namaste," Joy said, her voice carrying through the clearing. "Namaste," the crowd echoed.

As the crowd dispersed, Ember, Jade, Derek, and Frank stepped down from the platform.

Ember glanced at Jade, who offered a reassuring smile. "Well," Jade said, "that was... a lot."

"A lot," Derek echoed with a half-smirk. "But it's not every day someone declares you the hope of an entire community!"

Frank gave a low bark, padding closely beside Ember as they walked. The tension in her shoulders softened at his presence.

They followed the winding trail back to their tents, the hum of the yoga class fading into the rustle of leaves and the distant chirping of birds. Every person they passed nodded respectfully or murmured quiet words of encouragement. Ember felt a swirl of emotions—overwhelmed by the enormity of what lay ahead yet steadied by the sense of unity around her.

At their tents, they each took a moment to process and prepare. Frank stretched out at Ember's feet, his ears twitching at the sounds of the forest.

Before long, Joy appeared. "It's time," she said.

They gathered their belongings and began the walk toward the trailhead. The forest seemed quieter now, as though it, too, was holding its breath.

When they reached the trailhead, a group was already waiting in silence. Ember, Jade, Derek, and Frank stood together in front of the group, their figures framed by the towering trees, ready for what lay ahead.

Another healer came forward from the group and pressed a small jar into Jade's palm. "Smelling salts. Always good to have on hand."

Then an elderly man stepped forward, leaning heavily on a knotted walking stick. His frail hands cradled something small, and his gaze seemed to pierce straight through Ember. As he reached her, he extended his hand, revealing a smooth, polished stone with a divot worn into its surface.

"This belonged to your mother," he said, his voice rasping with age. He pressed the stone into her palm, his grip surprisingly strong. "She used it to center herself. She'd want you to have it now."

Ember stared at the stone, her thumb instinctively finding the groove. She rubbed at it, the surface cool against her skin. "How did you—"

The group of people approached all at once, no longer waiting their turn.

The man shook his head, cutting Ember off. "Just keep it close," he said. Then, he turned and shuffled back into the crowd, disappearing as quickly as he had come.

Before Ember could process the encounter, Derek leaned in with a lopsided grin. "Oh, that's the local mediumship guy— deep into all that spirit talk. He probably had a chat with your mother this morning," he said. "Don't overthink it—but keep the stone. It's a good one."

Ember blinked at him, still holding the stone, before sliding it into her pocket with a small nod. "Right. Sure."

A young woman then stepped forward.

"Brianna?!" Ember blinked. "Of course you're here."

A warm smile lit her face. "I was hoping you'd make it." Brianna said.

Ember stepped closer. New Age Barbie, she'd called her back in the studio—taupe hoodie, glossed lips, all heart-space and light frequencies. But here...

Brianna was a picture of strength and grace, her long, dark hair pulled back into a loose braid. She carried the subdued energy of someone who didn't need attention yet drew it effortlessly—her vibe intriguing and mysterious. The kind of woman everyone wanted to know more about.

"That day in class," Ember said. "When you talked about the cave and the pull. I thought maybe I was imagining things. But you knew."

"I saw that you'd had a glimpse too," Brianna said, her voice steady. "It was in your eyes. Coming here, even for a moment, it changes you."

Ember nodded, something loosening in her chest. "I thought I was losing it." She paused. "But when you spoke, I didn't feel so alone."

They stood for a moment, grounded in the knowing between them. No pretense. No performance. Just two people who had seen the same impossible thing and were finally standing in it together.

Brianna broke the silence with a smile, then reached out and gave Ember's arm a gentle squeeze. "You're not alone in this."

She turned to Derek, took his hands in hers, and said softly, "You better come back." A hint of warmth in her voice. "I'll be thinking of you." Then she let go, gave them both a small nod, and walked back toward the larger group,

Jade gave Derek an exaggerated look and rolled her eyes knowingly.

Even Frank received a gift when a child ran up to tie a bright scrap of fabric around his neck like a bandana. Frank wagged his tail proudly.

Finally, it was Joy's turn. She approached the group, her hands cradling a bundle of small woven bracelets. Each one was unique, crafted from vibrant threads and woven in intricate patterns. Tiny beads, no larger than a grain of sand, dotted the designs, and shimmered in the light. At the center of each bracelet was a single larger bead—smooth, iridescent, and glowing as though holding a spark of life.

"Before you go," Joy said, "take these. They're not just bracelets, they're your mats. They'll stay with you, light as air, until you need them."

Ember reached out and took the bracelet Joy offered her. The threads—gold, blue, and crimson— were warm to the touch, and the center bead seemed to pulse against her palm. "How does it work?" she asked, turning it over in her hands.

"When you need your mat, tug on the center bead and focus on your breath. It will unfurl. It will know when you're done and return to your wrist. No matter how far you travel, now, home will always be with you."

Jade slid her bracelet on and studied its design. The threads created a pattern of green and violet vines winding around her wrist, accented by beads that glowed like dew drops. "It's beautiful," she said, her voice reverent.

Derek bent down and rested his crystal sword against his shoulder, freeing his hands. He tied his bracelet. It was bolder, its colors darker—charcoal gray with streaks of orange—and its center bead glinted like a drop of molten steel. "Convenient," he said, giving it a tug.

Joy stepped back. "Remember, these mats carry more than their physical form. They carry the intention, the grounding, and the connection of this community. Wherever you go, you are never alone."

Ember looked down at her bracelet, running her fingers over the threads. The way the colors and textures came together felt deeply personal. It felt like more than a token—it felt like a promise.

Ember looked at her companions. "Ready?"

The group nodded in unison, and with one final look back at the community that had gathered to see them off, they turned toward the trail.

Together, they took the first step, their feet crunching on the gravel path. The trail ahead twisted into shadowed woods and sheer cliffs, a daunting and treacherous climb.

Had they begun a journey—or a rebellion?

CHAPTER 18

SHADOWS
OF DISTRACTION

The trail steepened, winding through dense pines. The air grew cooler, carrying the earthy scent of moss and bark, sharp with a metallic sting to the senses.

"It's different now," Ember said, more to herself than anyone else.

Derek slowed and glanced back. "It's supposed to be. This is the part where it stops being an idea and starts being real."

Ember ran her fingers over the bracelet on her wrist for comfort. "Do you think they're watching us?"

Jade's eyes flicked to the trees. "The Watchmen? Maybe. Or maybe they're waiting."

"For what?" Ember asked.

"To see if we're worth the trouble," Derek said, smirking.

Frank let out an uncertain bark, and the group fell silent again. The forest was quiet; the only sound the steady crunch of their steps.

As the sun dipped lower, long shadows stretched across the trail. The path opened into a clearing.

"Look up there," Derek said, pointing.

Rising from the edge of a plateau stood something none of them had expected.

A structure that looked like an ancient ruin stood tall against the sky, its stone arches and columns weathered but imposing. The structure seemed alive, pulsing with an energy that set Ember's nerves on edge. Above it, four glowing orbs floated in perfect stillness, their colors swirling and shifting—violet, gold, and blue, like liquid light captured in motion.

The group froze, captivated. Ember felt an inexplicable pull towards them, her feet moving before she made the decision to walk. The others followed without a word, their breaths shallow, their movements careful. Frank padded beside them, his tail tucked and ears pinned back.

They reached the center of the ruin, where a massive flat stone slab dominated the space.

Jade paused, her eyes on the slab. "A Sun Circle," she said. "I've never seen one before."

The symbol on the stone was unmistakable—rays radiated outward from a central point, their edges worn by time but still sharp in their symmetry. The design seemed to pulse with an otherworldly glow, as though it carried the memory of a forgotten power, waiting to awaken. The pillars around the slab framed the darkening sky, streaked with deep purples and oranges, while the orbs hovered directly above, casting strange, shifting shadows across the cracked floor.

Ember stepped onto the stone and knelt, her fingers tracing the etchings in the slab. She looked up at the orbs, then lay back, flat against the surface. She studied them like a child watching the stars. The others followed, forming a loose circle with their heads nearly touching. Frank curled at Ember's feet, placed a paw over her foot, and lay unsettled and panting.

The orbs swirled; their movements deliberate but unpredictable.

"It's so beautiful," Jade whispered. "Hypnotizing."

Ember's focus narrowed. Her heartbeat quickened. There was something wrong—something clawing at the edge of her mind that she couldn't quite figure out. The orbs began moving faster, their rhythm becoming erratic.

Her stomach dropped.

"These aren't orbs," her voice quivered. "They're lures!"

The words had barely left her mouth when the air shifted. The pressure dropped, and the gravity around them intensified. Ember gasped as the invisible force pinned her to the stone, her limbs immobilized. The others jerked and struggled, but they couldn't move.

"What's happening?" Derek's voice was tight, strained against the crushing weight.

The swirling orbs above them began to spin faster, their colors darkening. They lost their shape and became warped. Frank began barking incessantly as a high-pitched buzz, like the sound of a drone, sounded and vibrated through the stone and into their bones.

The pillars stretched taller, twisting as though alive, their jagged tops scraping against the sky. The sky above seemed to recede, pulling farther and farther away until the view above became an endless void.

Frank whimpered; his body pressed flat. His claws scraped against the stone, but he couldn't move.

The orbs above aligned in pairs, pausing in eerie stillness, they turned black with a gold slit that opened and closed.

"Did they just blink at us?" Derek yelled.

The sound around them screamed, frantic, as the orbs burst apart in a blinding flash. Shadows poured from their centers, thick and oily, twisting and writhing like smoke given form. They grew larger, taking shape—elongated, humanoid figures with edges that shimmered and wavered as though caught between worlds.

Eyes of molten gold flickered open in the shadows, followed by jagged, bone-crushing grins. The air grew icy. Then came the laughter—guttural, rising into a maddening chorus of cackles that rattled the bones, echoing in every direction.

The shadows swirled above them, tightening into a vortex, and then began their descents. They dove lower, each descent sharper, more menacing. Smoke-like tendrils slithered from their forms, brushing against the stone and sending violent shivers through the group. One shadow stopped above Ember; its burning eyes locked on hers.

"You are nothing," it spat, venomous. A clawed hand lashed out, slicing the delicate space behind her ear. Ember felt the hot sting of the cut. Blood trailed down her neck in a slow, burning line. For a moment, the pain rooted her—until the fear came crashing in.

The shadows turned on the others, their whispers slicing through the air like blades.

"Insignificant," one sneered at Derek. "You'll die forgotten."

The words wrapped around them, suffocating, their weight pressing down like hands closing around their throats.

"You can't save them," another hissed, its smoky tendril curling behind Jade's ear, cold as death, its breath searing her skin. "You'll lose everything. Disease will follow you."

The shadows' words burrowed deep, sinking into their minds, feeding on their every fear, twisting it into a nightmare they couldn't escape.

The wind picked up suddenly, whipping through the ruin with a violent force. The shadows cackled louder, their laughter twisting into something manic.

Ember's chest tightened. Her thoughts spiraled. Then, something caught her eye—gold chain bracelets, clinking as the shadows moved. The style was unmistakable. She had seen it before. Dunn's.

The recognition hit her like a thunderclap, and with it came the surge of clarity and resolve. He had corrupted this place, twisted it into his own. She clenched her fists, nails digging into her palms, gathering the courage she needed.

"You KNOW nothing," she snarled, her scream cutting through the storm.

The shadows froze, their gold eyes narrowing. The ruin plunged into an oppressive silence. For seconds, the gravity holding them down eased. Ember felt the release and didn't hesitate.

"RUN!" she yelled, pushing herself off the stone.

Frank bolted first. His claws scrambling against the smooth surface before gaining purchase. Derek and Jade followed; their breaths ragged as they fled toward the trees.

The shadows shrieked in unison, their forms stretching as they gave chase. The wind howled, branches snapping, the forest swallowing them whole.

Ember ran harder, blood pounding in her ears. Derek and Jade were close behind, crashing through the underbrush, Frank's frantic barks guiding their way ahead.

Ember's foot caught on a root, and she stumbled, her hands scraping against rough bark as she caught herself. She didn't stop. She couldn't.

Ahead, the trees began to thin, revealing a faint glow. Ember pushed forward, her legs burning as she broke through the tree line. The group burst into an open expanse.

Ember's chest heaved as she turned back to Jade and Derek, who were doubled over, clutching their knees. Frank nuzzled Derek's hand. Derek reassured him with a pat.

The shadows, the whispers, the gold chains—this wasn't just fear. This was Dunn. He was controlling the shadows, using them to get into their heads, to weaken them.

"What was that?" Derek asked, his voice tight. "Did you hear those sounds? Were they... talking to you?"

Jade wiped her face, her hands trembling. "It felt like... they were inside my head. Like they knew everything."

Ember's gaze shifted to the trees, where the shadows had vanished.

"It was him," she said. "Dunn."

"What? How do you know?" Derek asked. "There are lots of strange things in Resonance that aren't necessarily Dunn."

"I saw a gold chain on the shadow. It was the same as the one I saw on Dunn at my parents' celebration of life."

Derek blinked, still trying to process. "So, he used the shadows to mess with us?"

Ember nodded. "He's controlling them, getting into our heads, making us doubt ourselves. It's how he works—never just physical power. He breaks you down from the inside."

Derek clenched his sword, his jaw set.

The fight had begun.

CHAPTER 19

HOLDING ON
AND LETTING GO

The group reached a narrow plateau just as the last traces of daylight dissolved into twilight. The mountains surrounded them, jagged and towering. Below, thick clouds clung to the valleys, blanketing the world in mist.

"This looks good," Derek said, dropping his sword. "Flat enough, and no signs of creepy orbs or shadows."

Frank sniffed the ground and sat, showing his approval.

"Frank is breathing funny." Jade remarked, her tone clipped.

Derek glanced at her with a frown. "He's just tired, Jade."

"Tired or tachycardic?" she muttered, leaning forward to look closer at Frank. Her fingers twitched, ready to check his pulse, but she stopped herself halfway. "Never mind," she said, sitting back and sighing.

Ember smirked. "You were about to check his pulse, weren't you?"

"Force of habit." Jade shrugged.

"Maybe it's all of us. We need to ground ourselves." Jade settled beside Frank and pulled out a small pouch. "After what just happened, we can't carry that fear into tomorrow."

Ember sat cross-legged next to Jade, hands resting on her knees. "It wasn't just fear, "she said, "They spat distraction, doubt. They wanted us to self-destruct."

Derek leaned against a boulder, eyes distant. "They almost succeeded," he admitted. "I couldn't move. Couldn't even think straight. It felt... hopeless. Like they'd already won."

Ember touched the cut behind her ear, the sting still sharp. "But they didn't win. We're still here."

Jade nodded. "And that's why we need to reset. Let it go. We can't let them take up space in our heads." She pulled out a bundle of herbs and braided her hair, tying the end with a strip of cloth. "Sit with me."

They sat in a loose circle, their backs to the mountainside. Frank rested his head on his paws, his eyes half-closed as if sensing the calm.

Jade lit the bundle of sage, the smoke curling upward in lazy spirals. She held it in her hands and closed her eyes, breathing deeply. The sweet, woodsy scent filled the air, cleansing them and carrying a calming, almost spiritual energy.

"Close your eyes," Jade began.

Ember and Derek did as instructed.

"Feel the ground beneath you. It's strong, solid—it's been here far longer than any of us, and it'll hold you. Let yourself sink into it, be supported by it."

"Now, breathe," Jade continued. "In through your nose… and out through your mouth. Slow, deep breaths. Let everything that just happened fall away with the exhale. There's nothing you have to carry right now."

The group breathed as one, the sound rhythmic and steady, blended with the rustling wind through the rocks. Ember felt her shoulders relax for the first time since the ruin, the tension in her chest easing with each breath.

Jade's voice softened. "Imagine you're sitting on a pool of yellow light, a warm puddle surrounding you. Dip your fingers in, feel its presence. Picture it sending roots deep into the earth, your roots connecting deep into the soil. Let it fill you, warm you, ground you."

Ember's chest rose and fell with the rhythm of Jade's voice.

"Now, imagine a beam of blue light shooting out from the top of your head, reaching up into the sky. With your yellow roots grounded in the earth, and the blue light reaching upward, feel yourself anchored. Unmoving. Safe. Strong."

"Picture the light connecting us now. See your yellow roots stretching out, merging with ours, and your blue light expanding, blending with ours. Together. Stronger together. Brighter together."

The three of them sat in silence for a moment, breathing in sync, the imagined light weaving between them. Frank shifted, letting out a contented sigh, as the warmth of their shared energy filled the space.

"Slowly begin to bring your awareness back to the present. Let the yellow and blue light fade, knowing you can return to it whenever you need. Feel your body again, the ground beneath you. And, when you're ready, open your eyes."

The silence lingered for a moment as they slowly came back into their bodies. Ember blinked, stretching her fingers. Jade looked around. "How's everyone feeling?"

"Peaceful." Derek smiled. Ember nodded, not yet ready to speak. The mountains stretching before them felt less daunting now, less like obstacles and more like guides.

"Rest," Jade said. "Tomorrow's another climb. Who knows what's waiting for us." They sat together for a moment longer, the stars above burning brightly. Ember glanced at Derek, then at Jade, and finally at Frank, who was lying on his back, paws hanging in the air, facing up at the stars. A warmth settled in her chest—determination, maybe even hope. Whatever came next, they would face it together.

The mountain waited.

CHAPTER 20

EVERYTHING THEY NEED

The morning sun spilled over the mountains, golden light cutting through the fading mist. Ember stretched and groaned as the chill of the stone beneath her pressed into her back. Derek's voice called from the tree line before she could fully sit up.

"Breakfast delivery!" he announced, grinning as he emerged from the forest, Frank at his side. Derek held a handful of berries, while Frank trotted proudly ahead, carrying a cluster of mushrooms in his mouth.

"Frank! You can forage?" Ember raised an eyebrow, impressed.

"Frank's got better instincts than I do," Derek said with a shrug, dropping the berries into Jade's waiting hands. "Besides, he hasn't killed us yet."

Frank deposited the mushrooms at Ember's feet, wagging his tail like he'd found treasure. Then he turned and sat on Ember's feet as he, too, admired his haul.

Jade inspected the mushrooms. "Safe enough. Let's eat and get moving."

They ate quickly, though Derek's attention seemed elsewhere. He sifted through the dirt at his feet, his movements deliberate. Nearby, Frank gnawed on a stick, occasionally glancing up to watch. Derek unearthed a bent, tarnished button with traces of a design. His face lit up as he held it up. "Ooh, look, Frank. A keeper!" he declared, flipping it between his fingers before tucking it into his pocket. Frank wagged his tail furiously, as if cheering him on.

As they packed up, Ember adjusted her bracelet, it glittered in the sunlight. She looked up at the trail ahead, winding and steep.

"Alright," Ember said. "Let's go."

Derek slung his sword over his shoulder. Frank ran up, nudging his head into Derek's palm, then gave it a lick before bounding ahead, his enthusiasm infectious. "Well, if this is how we're starting the day, I'm in for whatever comes next."

Jade paused, her gaze shifting upward. The wind carried an eerie, melodic hum from above. "Do you hear that?"

Ember tilted her head, straining to listen.

"It's coming from up there," Jade said, pointing to a cliff just off the trail.

Derek's hand tightened around his sword hilt, his expression hardening. "Guess we're about to find out."

The hum shifted, growing louder, more insistent—as if it was calling them.

CHAPTER 21

THE GOLDEN PALACE

The trail twisted, revealing a break in the dense trees. There, nestled against the cliffside, was a palace of glimmering gold cascading from the mountain itself. The palace appeared to grow organically from the rock, its smooth, flowing architecture defying gravity. Circular terraces jutted out, supported by sweeping golden columns, their edges adorned with lush greenery.

The group paused in awe.

"What is this place?" Jade whispered.

Ember's eyes were locked on this vision. The palace seemed to hum, creating a vibration that resonated deep in her chest. She glanced at the others. Derek's brow was furrowed, and Jade's usually confident expression was tinged with unease. Even Frank, typically bounding ahead, stood still at her side, his ears perked forward.

"Do you know what this is? Who lives here?" Ember turned to Derek, cutting through the spell.

Derek shook his head. "No idea."

Jade crossed her arms.

The hum grew louder, shifting into something melodic, into a hauntingly beautiful song. A woman's voice, rich and pure, wove through the air, filling the space between them and the golden palace. It wasn't just sound—it was a feeling, a pull, as though the melody beckoned them.

Come now, my darlings, step into the glow,
Leave behind worries, no need where you'll go.
Gold in the garden, sweet songs in the air,
A world full of splendor, beyond all compare.

"It's so beautiful," Ember said, her voice barely above a breath. "I've never..."

"Shh," Derek put a finger to his lips. "I want to hear it."

Follow the shimmer, the path bathed in light,
Where feasts fill your senses, with no end to delight.

"Path bathed in light," Derek stepped forward.

Jade grabbed his arm. "Are you sure this isn't a trap?"

Derek shrugged, his easy grin returning. "Dunn's at the mountain top. This doesn't feel like him. We've always known there are others in Resonance who aren't with us at the base festival. This has to be some of them." He gestured toward the palace. "I've heard stories—musicians, hikers, artists—people who've found their own way here without mats. Maybe this is another group. How fun, right? I've always wondered if it was true."

"You've heard stories? That's not enough. Let's just stay the course. The path is right here. Why risk it?" Jade pressed.

Derek turned to Jade, somber. "Because we need all the help we can get, Jade. Dunn's no small obstacle, and if this is another group... maybe they can help us. Strength in numbers. What if they've faced him before? What if they know something we don't?" He motioned toward the palace again. "We can't afford to ignore a chance like that."

Jade hesitated, her eyes jumping between Derek and the palace. Ember stepped forward, her curiosity already leading her feet. "He's right. Let's at least see who they are."

Derek grinned and headed toward the palace, with Frank trotting at his side.

Jade hesitated, then let out a resigned sigh. "You're going to get us killed," she muttered, following after them.

The group moved toward the golden palace. The song growing clearer with every step.

Lay down your sorrows, your fears disappear,
All that you've dreamed of is waiting right here.

The voice was mesmerizing, promising something just out of reach.

Come now, my darlings, just one little taste,
Life in abundance, no moments to waste.

Their reflections sprawled across the glass and gold as they approached. The palace loomed even larger, its curves and terraces catching the sunlight and throwing warm reflections onto the cliffside.

They entered through an arched doorway, the silence of the palace almost as striking as its grandeur. Inside, their footsteps echoed as they turned the corner and found themselves in an opulent kitchen. Vividly colored foods spilled across the counters. Bowls overflowed with ripe berries, their skins taut and glistening, while baskets brimmed with sprigs of fresh herbs. Loaves of crackled artisan bread lay alongside wheels of creamy cheese. A sweet scent lingered—honey, citrus, and a heady floral undertone.

Beyond the kitchen, glass doors opened onto a sprawling garden.

Come now, my darlings, step into the glow,

"She must be out there," Ember pointed to the garden as she stepped outside, the others following.

They all stopped to take in the view.

The garden hung in the air, stretching out over the mountain's edge. Below them, an endless sea of clouds swirled, broken only by the jagged peaks of mountains piercing through like islands. Trees dotted the landscape, their branches swaying in the wind. Golden light bathed the scene, making everything sparkle as if the world itself had been polished.

"This is unreal," Jade murmured, her eyes wide as she took in the expanse before them.

"Ethereal." Ember added.

Your place at the table is yours to bestow.

The song led them farther into the garden, where they saw her—a woman standing at the edge, facing the horizon. Her golden gown shimmered and revealed delicate patterns woven into the fabric. She was adorned with jewels of deep emerald, gold, and glinting black, some seemingly not part of any jewelry, as if they were simply pressed onto her skin. Her cascading brown curls framed an almond face that was both regal and inviting.

As they drew closer, the woman turned, her movements fluid. Her gaze settled on them, and she smiled. "Why, hello there," she greeted, her voice as rich as her song.

"Your voice, I've never heard anything like it." Jade blurted, her Peruvian accent slipping through in the rawness of her wonder.

Derek nodded. "Yeah, that was... incredible."

The woman laughed. "You flatter me," she said, raising her chin. "I'm Sirenna."

Ember looked around, scouring. "What is this place?"

"This," Sirenna swept her arms wide, "is a sanctuary of abundance. A palace of pleasures and possibilities, where every desire is met, and every comfort is yours for the taking." She gestured to the palace behind her, the light catching its gleaming edges. "We celebrate the art of living—feasting, creating, reveling in the best that life has to offer."

Derek frowned, glancing around. "Are there... other people here?"

"Oh, absolutely," Sirenna said with an easy laugh, brushing off the question with a wave. "Some are inside the palace, enjoying its many offerings. I know you found it quiet in there; that's what the palace was offering you. Somehow it has a way of knowing what you need. Anyway, others are out on the grounds exploring, pursuing their passions, or taking time for themselves. They'll all return this evening for the nightly feast. It's a time of connection and celebration, and you're welcome to join."

"A feast?" Derek's eyebrows lifted in intrigue. "That sounds amazing."

"It truly is," Sirenna purred, stepping closer. "You've come at the perfect time. A moment of respite before continuing your journey, perhaps?" Her eyes scanned them, assessing their exhaustion. "You've walked far, haven't you? Faced no small challenges?"

Jade placed her hands on her hips. "Not that far. We've just started, really. And what exactly is this community? You were singing earlier—are you all performers or something?"

Sirenna chuckled, the sound honeyed. "Oh, no. I mean, sure, some of us are musicians, but others are explorers, inventors, or creators. We're not any one thing. Everyone here has found their way—earned their place." Her smile widened, her tone almost conspiratorial. "Even Dunn."

The group stiffened at the mention of his name. "Dunn's been here?" Ember asked, suspicion lacing her words.

Sirenna's gaze didn't falter, her smile unwavering. "Of course. You didn't think he got to where he is by sheer grit, did you?" She let the question hang, her tone sliding into something more persuasive. "Even Dunn needed help—an edge. He came through here, just as you have."

Derek frowned. "An edge?"

Sirenna's expression grew sly, her voice dropping to a near whisper. "Strength. His own type of shortcut. The tools to outmaneuver his enemies and harness his power in Resonance. He got everything he needed to become what he is now."

The weight of her words settled over the group like a heavy fog. Ember's stomach churned. "And what are you saying?" she asked. "That we won't make it without this... edge?"

Sirenna tilted her head, her expression equal parts pity and indulgence. "I'm saying the mountain is unkind, my dear. Dunn already has every advantage, and he will stop at nothing to protect what he's built. You, on the other hand—" She gestured at the group. "You're walking into a battle unarmed, carrying only your determination and that lovely sword." She winked at Derek. "Admirable, but hardly enough."

"Battle? Wait—how do you know what we're up to?" Derek's eyes narrowed.

"You'd be surprised how fast word travels." Sirenna twirled her hand in the air.

"What is it you want?" Ember asked.

Sirenna's eyes gleamed. "I'll show you," she said, "But first, let me offer you something in return. You're walking a dangerous path, are you not? Climbing toward the mountain top to face a man who would see you broken."

They all nodded. Frank panted and looked up to Derek for direction.

"Why take the hard road when there's a better way? The mountain is treacherous, filled with traps and trials that will drain you before you ever reach Dunn."

"Yes, we know." Ember said impatiently.

"But there's a shortcut. A hidden path that bypasses much of the mountain. It can bring you close to the summit, stronger, faster, and better prepared to face him."

Derek's eyes lit up. "You have a shortcut? That changes everything."

"Exactly," Sirenna said, her voice velvet, endearing. "But such things don't come freely. You understand."

The group exchanged glances. "What do you mean?" Jade asked. "We don't have money here—we can't pay you."

Sirenna's laughter rang out, light and unbothered. "Oh, no, no, not money. Nothing so mundane. Come," she said, beckoning them with a graceful hand. "I'll show you."

With a glance at one another, they followed her deeper into the garden, the promise of answers—both intriguing and unsettling—pulling them forward.

CHAPTER 22

THE SOUL TOLL

The sun dipped low, casting a surreal golden glow across the garden. Before them stood a row of gleaming golden columns, tall and etched with intricate patterns and symbols. Vibrant wildflowers and lush greenery provided the perfect contrast. The air hummed, as if the columns themselves were alive and breathing.

Sirenna gestured toward them with a sweep of her arm. "This," she began, "is the gateway to all that the palace offers. Beauty, nourishment, enrichment... A life free from want or struggle." Her voice was smooth and hypnotic. "There's just one small price to pay. Nothing drastic, I assure you. Just place your hands on the column, and it will reveal your toll."

Ember furrowed her brow. She glanced between the shimmering columns and her companions. "And if we don't agree with what it says?"

"Yes? What are you asking, Ember?"

"If we don't agree with what it says, we're not bound, right?"

Sirenna's lips curled into a knowing smile. "You must be the lawyer," she said. "Of course, my dear. You are under no obligation. It's merely an invitation. The choice is always yours."

Ember hesitated, her thoughts swimming. Ever since arriving, she'd felt an uncharacteristic weariness tugging at her, her parents' deaths, the impossible responsibility of defeating Dunn thrust upon her, the shadows, the endless questions about Resonance—it all pressed down on her. Maybe this place was the reprieve she desperately needed.

"It can't hurt," she said, turning to Derek and Jade. "Right?"

Derek shrugged. "What's the worst that can happen?"

"I don't trust this," Jade said, her eyes scanning the garden. "It feels too... perfect."

Sirenna smiled, her expression warm but unreadable. "Perfect, perhaps. But why deny yourselves what might be the answer you've been searching for? Sometimes, the first step is simply letting go."

With a deep breath, Ember stepped forward. Derek followed in quiet intrigue, and then Jade, muttering something under her breath about the risks of shiny objects.

They approached their columns, the reflective surfaces distorting their images like liquid gold. For a moment, they exchanged uncertain glances. Then Ember nodded, a silent signal, and together they placed their hands on the columns.

The air stilled.

Ember's column was the first to react. The gold surface rippled under her fingers like molten metal before it solidified again, red-hot cursive lettering burning across its surface: INFERTILITY.

"What?!" Ember's voice cracked. She pulled her hand back as if burned, staring at the word in disbelief. "I thought I was going to have to cook dinner or something!"

Beside her, Jade let out a small gasp. Ember turned as Jade's column lit up, the word CANCER etched in glowing letters that seemed to pulse with a dark energy. She took a shaky step back, her lips parted in horror.

Derek's scream shattered the air. Ember and Jade turned to him. "Frank?!" His voice was raw, panicked. At his feet, Frank cowered, his tail tucked, whimpering. Derek's column bore the word BETRAYAL, its letters glowing in crimson, jagged strokes. Along with it came an illustration. The image formed before him, drawn in real time like a cave painting etched in lines of smoldering ember—Derek, his hand resting on Frank's head in a silent farewell, then turning away. Frank's eyes were wide with confusion as his leash was passed to a faceless figure cloaked in shadow. Derek staggered back from the column, shaking his head. "No," he muttered, "I wouldn't... I couldn't."

Ember turned to Derek, her heart racing. "What the hell is this?"

"It's the Soul Toll," Derek whispered in disbelief.

Ember froze.

Not punishment. Not cruelty for its own sake.

Each toll had been chosen with care to strike the part of them tied closest to who they were. Jade's healing turned against her. Derek's loyalty threatened through loss. Her own future, her ability to create, to carry life—offered up like a coin.

She didn't steal light. She made you hand it over.

"You're asking us to step into the jail cell and throw away the key?" Ember said. "To willingly hand over the things that matter most?"

She took a step closer. "Why? To break us? To make us surrender to you?"

The wind picked up, rustling the leaves around them. The garden, once bright and welcoming, now felt a bit dim and heavy.

Sirenna stepped closer, her presence unsettling. "You're overreacting. Everyone faces challenges, often without knowing they're coming. This is merely a glimpse. Forewarned is forearmed, after all."

As tension crackled between them, Sirenna's voice slipped into a haunting melody that filled the air like an invitation and a command all at once. Her words poured out like silk, wrapping around the group in an almost tangible embrace. The song's pull was irresistible, drawing them closer as if each note was crafted to soothe their fears and ignite their desires.

Oh, the climb is steep, and the air is thin,
But here's a place to rest and stay.
The world out there is cruel and grim,
Why struggle when there's an easier way?

From beyond the hillcrest, two figures appeared, gliding effortlessly toward them as though carried on the notes of the melody. Their gowns, like Sirenna's, but in shades of sapphire and amethyst. Jewels adorned their skin—not worn but embedded—glinting like stars in a twilight sky. The effect was dazzling, their presence mesmerizing and surreal.

They joined Sirenna without a word, their voices slipping into the melody like threads into a tapestry.

Linger, linger, stay awhile,
A world of wonders, yours to see.
No need to suffer, no need to strive,
Everything you want—just come to me.

The harmony they created was unearthly, a sound so tantalizing that it felt alive. Each note carried a promise—of release, of indulgence, of freedom from everything weighing them down.

Ember's breath caught. The fear that had gripped her moments ago was now a whisper, drowned out by the ache rising in her chest. The trio's song seemed to reach into her soul, plucking at her deepest yearnings. She felt a pull, not just toward the music, but toward the vision it painted—a life of ease, beauty, and fulfillment, unburdened by the impossible task ahead.

The melody swirled around her, a call offering more than escape. It offered answers, solutions, a world where struggle no longer existed.

The mountain looms with trials ahead,
But here, the air is soft and sweet.
Why chase the unknown with so much to dread,
When joy and plenty are at your feet?

The song swelled, the figures twirling around them, their movements hypnotic. The words wormed their way into Ember's mind, each promise of abundance and ease a tantalizing whisper. But beneath it all was a cold, empty undertone that made her stomach twist.

Linger, linger, stay awhile,
A world of wonders, yours to see.
No need to suffer, no need to strive,
Everything you want—just come to me.

As the final note hung in the air, Sirenna turned to them, her smile radiant. "Of course, you'll stay."

Ember's jaw tightened. She stepped forward. "No."

Sirenna blinked, taken aback for the first time. "No?"

"No," Ember repeated, her gaze steady. "Whatever this is, I'm not trading anything for it."

Jade and Derek moved to stand beside her, their stances mirroring her resolve. Sirenna's smile twisted.

Derek unsheathed his crystal sword in one fluid motion, the blade scattering light in fractured shards. He leveled it at Sirenna, his voice steady. "Get out of our way."

Sirenna arched an eyebrow, her calm entirely unshaken. "Oh, how charming," she said, her voice dripping with mockery. "Do you think that pretty little sword of yours can scare me?" The trio laughed in unison; their amusement palpable. "You all think you're heroes, don't you? Marching into my domain with your shiny toys and hollow resolve."

The ground beneath them began to rumble, a low, ominous vibration that grew stronger with each passing second. Ember felt it through the soles of her boots, a tremor that signaled something was very wrong.

Sirenna stepped forward; her face turned cruel. "You have no idea what you've just done."

"Look!" Derek shouted, pointing at the golden columns.

The towering structures that once stood regal and solid now swayed like fragile reeds. Frank barked furiously, his paws skittering on the ground as he backed away. Cracks spiderwebbed across the polished gold, shards splintering off in flashes of metallic light. With an earsplitting groan, the first column toppled, crashing into the earth with a force that shook the entire garden. One by one, the others followed, shattering into jagged pieces that scattered like shrapnel.

The garden drained of its beauty, the flowers wilting in an instant. The air became charged with something dark and suffocating.

Ember turned back to Sirenna.

She no longer looked like the elegant, golden figure who had greeted them with open arms. Her beauty had twisted into something feral and menacing. Her once-smooth hair now whipped around her face in an unnatural frenzy, like tendrils of smoke. Her golden gown had darkened, its fabric now resembling scales, and her eyes—once warm—blazed with a fiery orange, the whites completely gone. A jagged scar stretched across her cheek, and her lips curled into a snarl, revealing sharp, animalistic teeth.

The palace behind Sirenna had transformed too. The smooth, golden curves had turned jagged and angular, its surface blackened like scorched metal. Windows were barred, and the once-inviting terraces now jutted out like cruel spikes. The structure no longer seemed like a sanctuary; it was a prison, its walls pulsing with sinister energy.

Sirenna's voice was low and venomous as she stepped forward. "You fools," she spat. "You think you're better than me? You think you can DO better than me?" Her voice rose to a piercing shriek. "Idiots! You won't make it another day out there without me!"

The forms of the women who had sung beside Sirenna twisted and stretched. Their limbs elongated, gowns darkened, the fabric splitting and shifting like scales. Hair whipped around their faces, eyes burning the same fiery orange as Sirenna's.

The final columns crashed down around them, and the ground buckled, forcing the group to stumble backward. Ember's heart raced as she grabbed Frank's collar, pulling him close.

With a sudden, predatory lunge, the women sprang forward, chasing after them with inhuman speed.

"Run!" Jade yelled, already darting toward the trail.

The group bolted, the earth trembling beneath their feet as Sirenna's screams echoed through the air. The garden they had walked through so calmly earlier now seemed a labyrinth of danger, the once-clear path twisting and strewn with debris.

A sudden burst of green light flared across the sky. Ember risked a glance back. The transformed women faltered mid-stride, heads snapping toward the palace. Another pulse of green light flashed, and the women veered away, racing back toward the source.

Ember's caught another flash of green light, it came from the basement window of the palace. Her steps faltered for half a second as she saw men in suits—dozens of them—streaming into the room through the walls, parachutes strapped to their backs like they had just descended from the sky. Their movements were mechanical, coordinated.

"Ember, come on!" Derek yelled, snapping her attention back.

They tore through the final stretch of the garden. As they reached the trailhead, Ember cast one last glance over her shoulder. Through the cracked palace windows, she saw the green flash again—brighter this time.

Ember couldn't shake the feeling that Sirenna's wrath wasn't the worst thing they'd encountered. Not yet. Something far bigger was coming, and it was already here.

CHAPTER 23

HELLO TO ALL SELVES

The group found a quiet cave tucked into the mountainside, the chaos of the golden palace and Sirenna's rage now a distant rumble in their minds. The echo of wind through the stone offered a soothing contrast to the firestorm they'd just escaped. Derek and Jade sat together, calming their breath as Frank curled at their feet.

Ember dropped to a seat on a large rock and tugged off her boots. She pressed her bare feet to the cool, uneven dirt, curling her toes into the rough patches of grass and stone.

Jade arched a brow, and untied her braid for the third time in as many minutes. "Careful you don't roll an ankle on those rocks, Ember. Not much I can do for you out here."

"Grounding. It's a thing," Ember replied, deadpan. Her voice softened as she stared down at her feet. "Reminds me I'm still here."

Derek snapped softly, a quiet sound that seemed more for himself. "You know, sometimes it feels like everything here tests you," he said, tilting his head, "but maybe that's the point."

"I'll be back in a bit." Ember offered as she stood and wandered deeper into the cave, seeking solitude.

She settled on a smooth rock near the edge of another opening, her gaze falling to the valley below. Sunlight draped the lush expanse in warm hues, but she barely saw it. Her thoughts churned as she whispered to herself, "That was intense."

She traced the ridge of the worry stone in her pocket. Her thumb pressed into the groove. "Is the extraction of your soul really that straightforward?" she murmured, the words weighted with disbelief. "How have I not seen it that way before?" The question hung before her, unanswered but pressing.

Ember closed her eyes and leaned her head back against the stone. A sudden calm washed over her, and she found herself standing in a void—soft, infinite, and shimmering with white light.

Before her appeared a younger version of herself, no more than eight years old, barefoot and wild-haired, clutching a flower she had likely plucked from some forgotten field. The child looked up at her, eyes wide with wonder. Beside her emerged another version of herself—Ember, caught in the grind of her corporate life. This version wore tailored clothes and carried a sense of exhaustion, her shoulders tense as if perpetually bracing for impact. Finally, a third figure appeared. It was herself as she was now in Resonance: weary, yet alive with a fire of determination.

They stood in silence, regarding one another.

"I'm sorry," Ember whispered, her voice trembling. "I'm sorry for losing my way. For forgetting you—forgetting me."

She turned to her younger self. Her chest tightened. "I forgot how to dream." Her eyes shifted to her corporate self. "I let the grind define me, take from me." And finally, to her Resonance self. "But I'm here now."

Her younger self stepped forward and placed the flower in her hand. Her corporate self gave a tired smile, and her Resonance self nodded, as if to say, *We knew you would remember.*

Ember stood taller, the flower cradled in her palm. The void faded as she opened her eyes to the cave once more, the valley stretching before her. The weight that had settled in her chest earlier seemed lighter now.

She emerged from her solitude, her steps measured and her resolve clear. Derek and Jade looked up as she approached, sensing the change in her.

"You good?" Derek asked, his tone unusually gentle.

Ember nodded, a small but determined smile tugging at her lips. "Yeah," she said simply. "Let's keep going."

CHAPTER 24

BREAKING THE CHAINS

The room was cloaked in shadow, lit only by the flicker of a single low-hanging bulb that cast jagged, ominous shapes across the walls. At the far end of a long, polished table, Dunn sat, his presence as imposing as the heavy gold chain resting on his chest. The chain glimmered, catching the scarce light like a predator's gleam. His tailored black suit, sharp and pristine, contrasted with the weathered lines of his face—a mask of control, cunning, and something colder lurking beneath.

Opposite him, Hector leaned forward, hunched and skeletal, his bony hands clutching at the table's edge. His suit hung awkwardly on his wiry frame, his sunken eyes darting nervously between Dunn and the shadows as though expecting them to spring to life. A bead of sweat trailed down his temple, but he dared not move to wipe it away.

"Sir," Hector began, his voice trembling, like the strings of a marionette pulled too taut. "Ember... she's begun the ascent."

Dunn didn't look up immediately, his fingers steepled in thought. When he did, his gaze was a blade. "Is she alone?"

"No, sir," Hector stammered, shifting uncomfortably under Dunn's scrutiny. "She has two others with her... and a dog."

Dunn's lips curled into a cold smile, but it didn't reach his eyes. "And?"

"They—they just passed the Soul Toll," Hector continued, his voice barely above a whisper. "They didn't take it."

The silence that followed was deafening. Dunn tilted his head, considering this revelation, and then leaned back in his chair. A low, guttural laugh bubbled up from his throat. "They think they can do it on their own." He shook his head, his grin widening into something almost wolfish. "The hubris." Still, he made a mental note. Roland wouldn't like the deviation.

Hector watched, wide-eyed, as Dunn's fingers drummed against the table, each tap reverberating like an unspoken threat. "Just keep me updated," Dunn said finally, dismissively.

"Wait," Dunn ordered, halting Hector mid-scramble toward the door. His voice dropped to a dangerous, deliberate tone. "Does she have her light?"

Hector froze, his eyes flickering with panic. "That... I don't know, sir."

"Well, find out!" Dunn barked, the sudden ferocity in his voice slicing through the room like a whip. Hector practically tripped over himself as he scurried away, disappearing into the shadows beyond the door.

Dunn let out a long breath, leaning forward again. His fingers traced the edge of the chain around his neck as he glanced toward his cronies seated around the table, their faces obscured by the dim light. They said nothing, but their presence was palpable—watchful, waiting.

He broke the silence, his tone casual but laced with menace. "This should be entertaining. Let her climb. Let her think she's getting closer. It only makes the fall more satisfying."

Outside, the wind howled against the mountain's peak, as if carrying a warning too late to be heard.

CHAPTER 25

GREEN LIGHT
IN THE SHADOWS

The trail narrowed, winding through a vibrant expanse of wildflowers and lush greenery. Mountains towered in the distance, their peaks brushed with the first hints of snow, while the valley below lay cloaked in a soft, shifting mist. Birds called out to one another in the stillness, their songs momentarily breaking the quiet as the group trudged on, their boots crunching against the rocky path.

Derek was the first to break the silence, his voice light but tired. "So, just to recap," he began, glancing at the others, "we ran from an ancient, soul-collecting palace after rejecting a toll from a woman who can apparently sing the sense out of your head."

Jade snorted. "Don't forget her disappearing backup singers. What was with that?" She gazed ahead, distant, and still processing. "Do you think they were real?"

"Real enough to feel like we were walking into a trap," Derek replied. "Good thing we didn't linger."

Ember stayed quiet for a moment, her thoughts tangled. The image of the green flash she'd seen in the basement window replayed in her mind, vivid and unsettling. She cracked her neck—one side and then the other— and cleared her throat, finally speaking up. "There's... something else." Both Derek and Jade turned to her. "When we ran past the palace, I saw something through a window. A green light."

"Green light?" Derek raised an eyebrow, curiosity flickering in his expression. "What kind of light?"

"It wasn't just light," Ember said carefully, trying to piece it together. "It looked like... people. Men in suits. They were just streaming into the room, through the wall, and they—" she hesitated, "they were wearing parachutes."

Jade stopped in her tracks, her brow furrowed. "Parachutes? In Resonance? That doesn't make any sense."

"None of this makes sense," Derek pointed out as he started walking. "But if Sirenna's place is a hub for all kinds of people, maybe it's connected to Dunn somehow? Maybe he's... importing people?"

"That's a leap," Jade muttered, though her tone wasn't entirely dismissive. "But it's weird enough to be true."

"I don't know what it means," Ember admitted. "But it didn't feel right. Whatever it is, we need to keep moving. If Dunn's involved, we're already behind."

The group fell silent again, the weight of what they'd seen and the uncertainty ahead pressing down on them. The trail curved, and as they rounded the bend, a gust of wind swept through the valley, carrying with it the faintest hum—so faint it could've been a trick of their minds.

Jade shook her head. "Sirenna, parachutes, green lights... it's like this place keeps rewriting the rules."

Derek gave a small, humorless laugh. "Rules? If Resonance has rules, I'd love to know them." He placed his hand on the hilt of his sword, "I thought I had some power in this sword. It felt so real, but apparently that's another trick of this place, or of Dunn, or—I don't know. I feel like an idiot."

Ember placed a hand on Derek's shoulder and leaned into him. "Don't get discouraged, that's *their* most powerful weapon. You felt something in this sword, Derek." Ember placed her hand on his. "We will figure this out, too. For now, we don't have to know all of the rules of the game," Ember said, her gaze fixed ahead. "We just need to keep going."

Derek nodded. "Keep going where, though? The mountaintop feels farther with every step, and we've got nothing but questions."

Jade exhaled, her shoulders stiff. "If this place is going to keep throwing surprises at us, we need allies. Sirenna's not the only one out here. There's bound to be others."

A silence settled over them, the trail narrowing as the trees thickened. The air carried a strange stillness. Then, the sound of voices—muted but unmistakable—drifted through the trees ahead.

Ember stopped in her tracks, her eyes narrowing as she scanned the path. "Do you hear that?"

Jade stiffened. Derek tilted his head, his expression cautious but curious. "Voices," he murmured, his tone edged with both wariness and hope. "Not Sirenna's singers this time."

The hum of conversation grew louder as they stepped forward, each sound a thread weaving into something bigger—something alive. Frank barked softly, his ears perked, his nose twitching.

"Let's hope these surprises don't come with scales or songs." Jade added.

Ember's heart raced as the forest began to thin again, revealing shadows moving just beyond the next ridge. "We'll find out soon enough," she said, resolute.

The group exchanged glances, then pressed on, the tension thick as they drew closer to whatever—or whoever—awaited them ahead.

CHAPTER 26

THE WANDERERS

The mist thickened as they ventured deeper, curling around the group like unseen hands. The air carried a strange hum—not music, but the fragments of something once whole. It wasn't long before they saw the figures moving in the haze.

At first, they seemed like shadows, flickering between the trees. Then the Wanderers came into focus. Their faces were a kaleidoscope of expressions: vacant stares, serene smiles, furrowed brows. Some moved with dreamlike slowness, as if wading through water, while others jerked about in sudden, chaotic bursts. A woman stood with her arms outstretched, her head tilted back as if basking in the sunlight that wasn't there. Nearby, a man was tracing circles in the dirt with a stick, muttering under his breath.

"They look…" Derek trailed off, his voice barely a whisper. "Like ghosts."

"Not ghosts," Ember said firmly. But the unease in her voice betrayed her. She stepped forward, her gaze fixed on a man who was rocking gently back and forth, humming a tuneless melody. "They're alive."

Jade grabbed her arm. "Alive or not, they're not all there. Don't get too close."

Ember shook off her grip. "We can't just leave them like this."

She approached the man, her footsteps careful. "Hello?" she called, her voice cutting through the mist. "Can you hear me?"

The man stopped rocking, his eyes snapping to her with startling intensity. "Hear you?" he repeated, his tone light and distant. "Yes, yes, I hear everything. The trees, the wind, the stones whispering secrets."

"What happened to you?" Ember asked, kneeling to meet his gaze. "Why are you here?"

His face twisted into a look of exaggerated thoughtfulness. "Why am I here? Why are any of us here?" He laughed softly, almost melodically. "The path was too long, too heavy. So we stayed. We forgot. But it's fine, you see. Fine, fine, fine." His voice rose, almost sing-song.

Ember pressed on. "Forgot what? How did you get here?"

The man didn't answer. Instead, he turned his gaze skyward and began humming again, swaying gently.

"Excuse me!" Ember called out to another Wanderer, a woman with streaked hair and torn clothing. The woman's lips moved, forming words without sound, her hands miming some invisible task.

Ember reached for her shoulder. "Please, tell me—how can we help you?"

The woman's hands paused midair. She turned to Ember with an almost childlike smile. "Help? Help, help. Do you have honey? Or stars? Maybe clouds wrapped in lace?"

"What does that even mean?" Jade muttered, watching the woman twirl away, giggling softly.

"This is pointless," Derek said, his voice tight, his hands clenched into fists. "They're gone, Ember. Whatever they were before… they're not coming back."

Ember refused to accept that. "No. There's got to be a way. They're still here. They're just… lost."

Before Derek could retort, a soft, choking sound from one of the Wanderers caught Jade's attention. Her head snapped toward the source, and without hesitation, she approached.

"Jade, don't," Derek warned.

But Jade's instincts had already kicked in. She crouched down beside the emaciated figure, her fingers reaching for his wrist. Her brow furrowed as she murmured under her breath, "Tachycardic… definitely hypoxic." The man turned glassy eyes toward her, muttering something incoherent before stumbling away. Jade stood, brushing her hands on her pants, her jaw tight. "They're barely functioning," she said.

Ember turned to another Wanderer, a young man crouched low to the ground, his hands clutching his head. "How can we help you?" Ember asked again, her voice steady despite the storm of emotion inside her.

The man didn't respond, didn't move. And then, slowly, he lifted a single trembling hand and pointed up—toward the peak of the mountain, hidden in the swirling mist. His finger remained fixed as his lips parted, whispering a single word: "Up."

The word hung in the air, heavy and final. Ember swallowed hard, her chest tightening.

"Up?" she repeated. "What's up there?"

But the man offered no more. He lowered his hand, his gaze drifting aimlessly once more. The others began to shuffle away, their movements as disjointed as their thoughts. The fragmented hum resumed, rising and falling like a dissonant chorus.

Jade stepped closer to Ember. "I think that's all we're going to get out of them."

Derek stared at the man who had pointed, his jaw tight. "Is that what happens to us if we fail? Is that what we'll become?"

Ember turned back to the trail, her eyes narrowing with determination. "Only if we let it." She glanced at Derek and Jade. "We keep moving. We don't stop. Not until we reach the top."

The group pressed forward, leaving the Wanderers behind. But the haunting hum lingered in the air, wrapping around their thoughts like a warning of what could come.

CHAPTER 27

ONLY FORWARD

The trail opened to a breathtaking overlook, sunlight breaking through the mist and casting the valley below in a soft, golden glow. Jagged cliffs framed the view, the expanse stretching endlessly toward a distant mountain peak that pierced the sky like an ancient sentinel. The mountain top, their destination, shimmered, as if it beckoned them forward.

Derek, Jade, and Ember stood side by side, Frank padding a step ahead, his ears twitching at every faint sound. The air was thinner here, lighter, but Ember's chest felt heavier than ever.

Her gaze lingered on the path behind them, where the Wanderers still meandered aimlessly, shadows in the mist. She clenched her fists, frustration tightening her jaw. "There has to be something we can do."

Derek, leaning on his knees to catch his breath, straightened and shook his head. "Ember, we can't save everyone. You saw them. They're... gone."

"No one's ever really gone," Ember countered, her voice sharp. "They're stuck, Derek. Not dead."

Jade gestured toward a clearing, where the Wanderers were out of view, and sat down. The group followed Jade's lead, sitting around her. Jade exhaled slowly, her arms crossed. "And what do you suggest? We carry them up the mountain? They can barely lift their heads."

Ember turned to face her, a mix of anger and desperation flashing in her eyes. "So we leave them to rot? To wander forever?"

"They made their choices," Jade said, her tone firm but not unkind. "Whatever happened to them, it started long before we got here. You can't undo that."

Ember looked to Derek for backup, but he avoided her gaze, staring at the peak in the distance instead. "Jade's right," he said reluctantly. "We're barely holding it together as it is. If we stop now, we're done for."

Frank whimpered, pressing his body against Derek's leg as though seeking comfort from the tension in the air. Ember rested her elbows on her knees and stared at the uneven ground in front of her, her fingers itching for something to do. She spotted a few twigs scattered near her boots and began gathering them, sorting by size without thinking. Short twigs to the left, longer ones to the right. She snapped a few in half, the sharp crack satisfying something deep inside of her.

Derek absently scratched Frank's ear, his eyes distant. "If we don't keep moving, we'll end up just like them."

Ember's breath hitched at his words, because she knew they were true. The Wanderers' hollow faces flashed in her mind, their eerie detachment a stark reminder of what could happen if they faltered. The image crushed her natural inclination to argue.

Jade broke the silence. "We have to focus on the mountain. Whatever's up there might be the only thing that can change any of this."

Ember nodded slowly, though it felt like defeat. "Then we don't stop," she said quietly. "For them, for everyone—let's make sure this isn't for nothing."

The group stood and faced the summit ahead, their silhouettes etched against the expanse of blue sky and rugged terrain. Derek glanced at Ember, his voice softer now. "We can't save them, Ember. But maybe we can stop anyone else from ending up like them."

Her throat tightened, but she didn't respond. Instead, she took a step forward, then another, the weight of her guilt and determination propelling her onward. Frank trotted alongside her, his loyalty a small comfort.

As they continued, the air grew cooler, the sun casting long shadows over the jagged cliffs. Behind them, the faint sounds of the Wanderers' murmurs faded into the distance, swallowed by the wind. Ember clenched her fists, the memory of those lost souls burning in her mind.

Ahead, the mountain loomed larger, its peak shrouded in a haze of mystery and promise. Whatever awaited them there, it had to be worth the sacrifice. It had to be.

CHAPTER 28

SPIDER WEBS

The trail dwindled, dusk wrapping the forest in a thick, oppressive gloom. The trees seemed to huddle closer together. Ember led the way, her steps deliberate, eyes trained on the ground for hazards she could control—roots, rocks— but the real threat hung invisibly ahead.

The first webs caught her off guard, fine gossamer threads brushing across her face. She swiped them away, rolling the silk into tiny balls between her fingers before flicking them aside. It wasn't the feel of the webs that bothered her—it was the growing sense of entrapment, like the forest was closing in on them.

"Watch your head," she called back over her shoulder as she released a branch and glanced at Derek and Jade trailing close behind. Frank, trotting just ahead of Derek, let out a sharp sneeze as another strand grazed his muzzle. His ears flicked in irritation.

As they pressed on, the webs grew thicker still, the forest darkening as the canopy overhead became a tangled maze of silk. The forest was quiet except for their labored breathing and the occasional curse as someone pulled at a particularly

151

stubborn strand of webbing. The once faint hum of insects and birds had faded into silence, leaving only the sound of their footsteps and the almost imperceptible rustle of the webs as they moved through them.

The webs thickened, draping across the path like veils. Ember grabbed a branch from the ground, holding it like a staff and spinning it in front of her to clear a path. Sticky, clinging threads twisted around the branch as she worked, but the webs seemed endless.

"This is disgusting," Jade grumbled, tugging a strand from her arm and flinging it away.

"Could be worse," Derek said, forced and thin. "No spiders yet. Just... empty webs."

"Yeah, that's *definitely* better," Ember deadpanned, holding up her branch, now encased in a gooey mass. She tossed it aside and grabbed another, unwilling to let her pace falter.

The sticky strands were everywhere now, forming dense, tangled barriers. Each step forward was a careful gamble, a futile effort to avoid the clinging webs that seemed determined to latch. The air was humid and heavy, carrying an ancient scent, as if it had lingered here for centuries, warmed and trapped within the swaddle of webs.

"We're past the point of this being cute," Ember snapped. "Brace yourselves and push through. Thrust out your chest. Own it."

"*Own it?*" Jade arched a brow and tugged at a web stuck to her hair. "I'm a surgeon, not a linebacker." She gestured dramatically to the path. "Be my guest."

Ember rolled her eyes but didn't argue. She pressed forward, her arms tight to her sides as the webs clung to her like a second skin, wrapping her shoulders and legs. Her hair tangled in the mess, but she kept moving, refusing to stop. When she broke through, she turned to the others, strands of webbing trailing from her shirt like ribbons.

"Your turn," she said, brushing herself off as best she could.

Jade rolled her shoulders, gave a mock salute as she muttered something in Spanish, and pressed forward. "This is why I stayed in the operating room," she jabbed.

Even Frank lowered his head and trudged through, his tail tucked in reluctant resignation.

Derek hung back, silent, gripping a branch he hadn't yet used. His eyes scanned the weaving webs ahead, his jaw tight.

"You okay?" Ember asked, catching his hesitation.

"Yeah," he said, not meeting her gaze. But the sharp edge in his voice betrayed him. He hesitated for a breath too long, then forced a laugh. "Just... thinking about what's waiting on the other side."

"Ugh, *when* we get to the other side," Jade said, brushing her arms clean. "How long do we think that will be?" She paused, her gaze narrowing as she studied Derek. "You're sure you're good?"

Derek gave a tight nod, but his knuckles whitened around the branch.

"Derek, why don't you put the branch down and try your sword?" Jade offered to both distract him and lighten the mood.

Derek did as he was told. He placed the stick on the ground and unsheathed his sword, the jagged crystal readied to take on the delicate silk. He stepped forward to take the lead, but his movements lacked their usual swagger.

He took a few timid steps.

"Do you feel that?" Derek's voice was sharp with unease. He stopped in his tracks, his hands brushing over his arms. "It feels like the webs are... tightening across me."

The once-translucent strands were thickening, and beginning to glow with a golden light. They stretched and twisted in intricate patterns, weaving themselves over Derek's shoulders and arms like living vines.

"Body armor!" For a moment, Ember was hopeful. Maybe this was some kind of gift—a defense, she thought. Maybe this could help them.

Derek's eyes widened in horror. He let out a strangled cry and dropped to his knees, clutching his chest. "Get it off!" he screamed, panicked. "GET IT OFF!"

"Derek!" Ember shouted, rushing to his side as he collapsed to the forest floor, writhing in agony. The golden threads spread over him like molten metal, fusing to his clothes and skin. His cries echoed through the forest. Ember's stomach twisted with helplessness.

Jade was already beside him, her hands tearing at the strands encasing his body. "It won't budge!" she cried, her voice cracking with frustration. "It's like it's alive."

Ember gritted her teeth, her fingers clawing at the metal threads. They were warm—almost burning to the touch—but they didn't give. Instead, they seemed to tighten further, locking Derek in place as his screams turned hoarse.

"What do we do?" Ember cried, as she looked to Jade.

Jade's jaw clenched, her doctor's mind racing as she tried to assess the impossible. "I don't know!" she admitted, her hands steady as she fought to free him. "This isn't... I don't know what this is!"

Frank barked frantically, circling Derek as if he could bite through the golden prison that was consuming him.

Derek's breathing grew ragged, his eyes squeezing shut as tears streaked his face. "Make it stop," he whispered. "Please... make it stop. Make it go away."

Ember looked around desperately, looking for anything— any clue, any sign. She couldn't find one, so she brought her full attention back to Derek.

"DEREK!" Ember grabbed his face with both hands. "Stay with me. You're stronger than this, stronger than whatever this is," she insisted, fierce.

Ember's heart pounded.

Jade eyed Derek's sword, and her brow furrowed. The once vivid crystal now appeared dull, its surface lifeless and cloudy. Where it had once shimmered, it now seemed drained, like a dimmed star.

Derek's eyes flickered open, unfocused but holding onto her voice. "I can't..." he gasped, squirming and struggling under the force.

The webs pulsed with light, and Derek let out one last cry before his body stilled.

"NO!" Ember screamed, shaking him. "Derek, don't you dare!"

For a terrifying moment, everything was silent.

And in the growing shadows, the forest seemed to whisper.

"Have you felt it? These threads, tightening across your chest, holding you so fiercely? Have you asked yourself why they're here? Or simply wished them away? Perhaps they cling not to trap you, but to urge you to listen."

"I'm listening." Derek whispered, almost inaudible. And with that, his body seemed to relax entirely, sinking into the dirt as though surrendering to the earth itself.

"Derek!" Jade and Ember both yelled as Frank laid low next to him, sensing something in the distance.

The golden light dimmed, and the webs slackened. Ember and Jade watched, stunned, as the threads unraveled themselves from Derek's chest, falling away like wilted vines. He lay sprawled on the forest floor, his body trembling, sweat and dirt smudged across his face and arms. The intricate golden strands pulsed, wrapping him in an otherworldly glow. His breaths came in shallow gasps

Derek opened his eyes, glassy with exhaustion and bewilderment. "What just happened?"

Jade pressed her fingers to his wrist, checking his pulse with clinical precision, her own breath unsteady. "You're OK," she confirmed, her words releasing tension.

The air shifted, carrying a chill that rippled through the group. A shadow moved within the deepening dusk; its presence heavy.

Shadows danced on the edge of their vision and then a dark figure descended, its edges fluid like ink poured into water, and as the figure landed, it didn't strike the earth—it unfolded into light.

A woman stood before them. She was neither young nor old, her features fluid and ever-changing. Her robes shimmered black with gold and silver, like the interplay of night and firelight. Her hair twisted in defiance of gravity, an ethereal halo of tendrils, wild yet elegant. Her eyes—bright and knowing—scanned the group as though seeing through every layer of their being.

"I'm here to remind you that you are alive," the woman began, her voice resonant and calm, as though it carried the wisdom of centuries. She looked down at Derek, her expression neither kind nor cruel, but steady and resolute.

"Who are you?" Ember asked, stepping forward despite the tremor in her chest.

The woman tilted her head, a small smile on her lips. "I am Fayra. I am fear, made form. I've existed since the beginning—eternal, like light and shadow. I do not follow or flee; I rise when you are ready to see me."

The air grew warmer, thick with the scent of cedar and earth after rain. Ember and Jade froze, their instincts at war with their curiosity. There was no malice in the figure's presence. Only weight. Only purpose.

Derek's lips parted, but no words came.

Fayra's gaze softened, "I am that feeling in your chest that holds tightly to you, not to harm you, but to remind you of your truth." Her hand hovered over the golden threads still clinging to Derek's chest, and they fell away. He was free.

"Why did you do this to me?" Derek finally rasped. "Why does it hurt so much?"

"Because you needed a strong reminder of your heart's desire," she said. "You were wavering. Not trusting yourself. Crushed by your sword's defeat. You were leading with fear and wishing it away, instead of listening."

"What could you possibly have to say?" Derek's voice was bitter; his hands clutched the dirt beneath him.

"You are alive." Fayra said again. "I hold you to remind you that there's a part of you still aching to come alive. There is freedom you've forgotten how to fight for."

Derek's agitation increased as he made his way to stand. "Freedom? That's literally why we're here. What more do you want from me?"

"That's why they are here," Fayra corrected as she gestured toward Ember and Jade. "But you, Derek—you took this path to prove something. Your greatest fear is not failure, but insignificance. The thought of a life without meaning consumes you."

She stepped closer, her gaze piercing. "This fear does not serve you. Face it with courage. Release it. The more you stop trying to prove yourself, and start doing what truly calls to your heart for freedom and for joy, the more I'll let go of you."

Tears welled in Derek's eyes. "And if I can't?"

"The feeling you feel is not of fear, Derek. It is of love. Loving you deeply enough to help you remember what truly matters to you. Life isn't about proving yourself, it's about seeing what's already here, who's already with you." Fayra looked to Ember, Jade, and Frank, each in turn. "I know that love doesn't come so easily in your family, Derek, but it does in your heart."

Derek closed his eyes, his breathing even now, as though Fayra's words had unlocked something deep within him. The webs dissolved completely, fading into the ground as though they had never been. When he opened his eyes again, they were clear, and the shimmer of light returned to his sword.

He looked down to his sword and then up to Fayra. He stood tall with his chest out, proud.

"Face the darkness with courage. It exists to remind you of the light." Fayra smiled as she nodded towards Derek's chest, as it began to glow. Derek felt the warmth and overwhelming sensation of comfort spread across his torso, as Jade and Ember gasped, realizing what was happening.

Derek smiled with the ease of knowing; it all felt so natural. He was back.

"Fear is your guide, not your master." Fayra emphasized, and then turned to Ember, her presence growing even more luminous.

Jade stepped between them. "Then what about the Breathers?" she asked. "People like me. We're still trying. We haven't given up. Why haven't you helped us?"

Fayra met her gaze. "I do help you. I press close to you, too. But trying to restore your light is not the same as surrendering your fear," she said. "You still battle yourself. You fear what will happen if you fully let go." She paused. "And know this: even when your light returns, the dance is not over. You may stray. You may forget again. And I will return each time, pressing close, until you remember."

A silence followed—then Ember stepped in, her voice harder. "And the Wanderers?" she asked. "Why have you let them stay lost?" Ember's jaw clenched.

Fayra's gaze held steady, unshaken. "Because they are," she said. "The Wanderers have drifted beyond choice. I press close, I always do, but they are lost in their minds, and no longer in their bodies. They do not feel fear as you feel it. I cannot guide what no longer feels."

She moved towards Ember. "But you, Ember Brooke... you arrived awake. With your light intact. That is rare. Do you know why?"

Ember's breath caught. She had asked herself this question so many times, but hearing it now, spoken aloud, felt like a challenge she wasn't ready to face. "No," she admitted.

Fayra's expression softened, and she took a step closer. "Your family has walked these paths before. Long ago, your ancestors twisted the Prism to serve themselves—like Dunn has done now—and shattered their bond with Resonance and corrupted their connection to the light. That fracture has echoed through generations, drawing your family back to this place in search of redemption."

Ember's throat tightened. "And my mother?"

Fayra nodded, her smile bittersweet. "Yes, Ember, your mother has been here. Many times."

Ember smiled. Her heart filled with love. And then she whipped around to Derek, "See! I knew it. The old man at the bottom of the mountain wasn't full of woo-woo nonsense. He had known her! And he gave me..." Ember trailed off as she reached into her pocket and pulled out the worry stone. "This." She said, as she rolled it in her fingers with new meaning.

Ember looked up at Fayra, "Please, tell me more."

"Your mother began to heal the fracture. She resisted the distractions that consume so many and chose balance over dominance. You are here now because you carry her legacy forward. Something in the cosmos has called you—not because you are the only one capable, but because you are ready."

Ember shook her head, the weight of Fayra's words settling over her like a heavy cloak. "But why me? Why now?"

"Because you are willing and able to act. Right person, right place, right time. It's as simple as that. Right now, Resonance teeters on the edge of imbalance, and the light you carry—and now you, Derek—is essential to restoring it. This is not a gift, Ember, it's a responsibility."

Jade's voice cut through the stillness, sharp and practical. "And if we fail?"

Fayra turned her gaze toward Jade, her expression unreadable, her voice like a current flowing from the depths of time. "Failure is not the end. It is a shift. The darkness will swell, yes, and the light will wane, but neither will vanish. Both are eternal, locked in a dance older than memory." She stepped closer, her presence filling the space between them like a storm on the horizon. "If you falter, the balance tips. The light dims, leaving room for the shadows to spread. But even then, the light will not be lost—it waits, always waits, for another to rise and reignite it. Yet know this: the longer the darkness reigns, the harder the path becomes."

Fayra's voice softened, almost tender, yet still laced with gravity. "You are here not because you were chosen above all others, but because you are willing to carry what others have dropped. If you fail, others will rise. But ask yourself—what does the world lose while it waits for that rising? And what will you lose if you do not try?"

Fayra stepped back, her figure beginning to blur.

"Wait!" Ember called. "How do I finish what my mother had started?"

Fayra's voice echoed, distant but clear. "By trusting the light within you and letting it guide your path. You will not be alone."

With that, she dissolved into a swirl of light and shadow, leaving the scent of cedar.

Ember, Jade, and Derek stood motionless, their thoughts racing in the vacuum Fayra had left behind. Derek clutched his sword, its crystal now glowing and pulsing in time with his steadying breaths, the brightness spilling into the darkened trail.

Jade broke the silence, her voice low and measured. "She's gone." She looked at Derek first, then Ember. "Do you believe her?"

Derek wiped a hand over his face, his grip tightening on the hilt of his sword. "It wasn't about believing. It was about... knowing." He turned toward Ember, his eyes clearer, steadier than they had been since the journey began. "She's right. The fear—it's always been there, twisting everything. But now..." He paused, exhaling deeply. "Now, I think I know what to do with it."

Jade, ever practical, stepped closer and placed a hand on Derek's shoulder. "Good. Because this isn't over, and we're going to need that light." Her eyes softened for a fraction of a second, then sharpened again. "Both of you."

Frank nudged Derek's leg, his tail wagging as if sensing the shift. Derek knelt to rub the dog's ears, grounding himself in the moment.

Ember's gaze drifted upward, past the tangled webs now dissolving into the ether, past the towering trees that loomed overhead. Fayra's words reverberated in her mind: *You are here because you are ready.*

Without conversation, Ember pocketed her worry stone and they began to climb again. The light in Derek's chest grew steadier, its glow reflecting in the crystal of his sword. Ember's steps quickened, her heart pounding with something new—something fierce and alive.

Ready? Ember considered. The word felt both fragile and weighty, like glass balanced on the edge of a table.

•◆•

Far above, at the summit, a figure moved within the darkened stone fortress. Dunn stood at the edge of his domain, watching the glimmer of light far below. Like fireflies. His lip curled into a sneer, but beneath the disdain, an unease rippled through him.

The light had returned.

And it was coming for him.

CHAPTER 29

AURORA BOREALIS

The group had found their resting place on a rocky outcrop high above the forest, where the world seemed to fall away. The ridge jutted out over a sprawling valley, and in places the ground was softened by a thin blanket of moss and sparse grass. Below them, layers of jagged peaks stretched into the horizon. The faintest breeze swept through, carrying with it the crisp scent of alpine air, and above them, the night stretched wide and endless. It was the kind of place that made you feel both exposed and cradled at the same time, as if the universe had intentionally carved this spot for reflection.

Above them, the night sky unfolded in a sprawling canvas of stars, pinpricks of light in hues of blue and gold that seemed to pulse with the rhythm of their own breath. The horizon was alive with shifting curtains of green and violet—the aurora borealis, dancing as though it were painting the heavens in real-time.

Ember lowered herself onto the ground, her legs folded beneath her. The tension in her shoulders eased as she let her gaze drift upward, her thoughts quieter now. She didn't speak, but her mind churned with everything Fayra had said. Her mother, the Prism, the weight of this responsibility—was she really ready? The aurora reflected in her eyes, and she allowed herself to wonder if her mother had ever sat here, under this same light, feeling just as uncertain.

Jade sat nearby, absently tying her hair back for the third time since they'd stopped. Her hands moved automatically, but her gaze remained fixed on the sky. She wasn't one to dwell on the metaphysical, but even she couldn't deny the magnitude of what they'd witnessed. The aurora's glow cast shifting patterns across her face, and for a moment, she let herself feel small. Not insignificant—just part of something far greater than herself. She exhaled softly, a doctor's precision in even this smallest act of release, and she glanced at Derek.

Derek lay flat on his back, arms sprawled out as though he were trying to take up as much space as he could. The warmth of the newly restored light in his chest had faded to a gentle hum, but he could still feel it—a steady pulse, like a metronome, keeping him tethered. His sword rested beside him, the crystal glinting in the aurora's glow. He stared upward, his mind replaying Fayra's words about insignificance. They hadn't stung; they'd sliced clean through him, exposing the truth he'd long avoided. But now, as the aurora painted the sky, he felt the first hints of something else—a purpose that didn't demand proving himself to anyone.

Frank padded around the group, his nose low to the ground, sniffing out every stray scent. Occasionally, he stopped to glance at the sky, his ears twitching as if he, too, were captivated by the display. He finally settled near Ember, curling up beside her with a soft huff, his warmth grounding her as much as the earth beneath her feet.

No one spoke for a long time. The aurora borealis continued its dance, casting the ridge in waves of shifting light. It was as if the sky itself was reminding them—there is beauty, even in uncertainty.

Ember reached out to scratch behind Frank's ears, her voice breaking the quiet. "Do you think it's always been like this up here?" she asked, more to herself than anyone else.

Jade glanced at her, then back at the sky. "If it has, we were too busy to notice."

Derek let out a low laugh, the first in what felt like hours. "Maybe that's the point."

No one answered, but the silence that followed was different—softer. The group stayed there a little longer, under the watchful glow of the stars and the swirling aurora, gathering their strength for what lay ahead.

The group reluctantly left the ridge, drawn by the need for rest. They found a mossy nook near a quiet stream that wound through the rocks. The moss was thick underfoot, soft enough to cushion their aching bodies. The stream's steady murmur filled the air, its cool mist brushing against their skin. Frank circled twice before flopping down beside Ember, his head resting heavily on her leg.

Ember leaned back against a smooth stone, staring at the stream. The events of the day churned in her mind—Derek's light returning, the truth about her mother, and Fayra's cryptic warnings. She felt the weight of it all pressing down; she still had no plan on how to defeat Dunn. They were marching, unarmed and unprepared, into the unknown.

Jade stretched out on the moss with a long sigh, her eyes already drifting shut. Derek sat against a tree, his sword balanced across his lap, his eyes starting to close.

The stream whispered as they settled, its quiet rhythm unchanging, indifferent to their exhaustion.

Ember laid down and just before she let sleep take her, she caught a flicker of green light beyond the tree line. She sat up, her muscles tensing, but the forest remained still. It had vanished as quickly as it had come. Nothing moved. Nothing came closer.

She lay back again, her mind racing. Whatever was out there, it was waiting.

And so were they.

CHAPTER 30

SUNRISE YOGA

The morning light filtered through the trees as the stream nearby babbled with a gentle rhythm through the crisp air. The clearing was framed by the towering trees and their interwoven branches. It felt secluded yet expansive.

Derek stretched him arms overhead and winced. "I don't know about you, but after yesterday, I could use some yoga. Look at this place—it's like it's asking for it."

Ember raised a brow but smiled. "Alright, let's do it. Might as well loosen up before we hit the trail."

The clearing glowed with the warmth of morning light as Ember unclasped her bracelet. She ran her fingers over the intricate threads—gold, blue, and crimson intertwined. The center bead pulsed against her palm, just as it had when Joy first handed it to her. Joy's words echoed in her mind: *These mats carry more than their physical form. They carry intention, grounding, and connection.*

She tugged gently on the bead, inhaling deeply, and the bracelet began to unfurl. The threads unraveled in a slow, fluid motion, like silk in water, expanding and reshaping themselves into a full mat. Its surface was rich with the same patterns. As it settled onto the mossy ground, Ember felt the connection Joy had spoken of—the mat wasn't just a tool; it was a reminder, a piece of home she carried with her.

Next to her, Jade held her bracelet, hesitating. "It feels alive," she murmured, tracing the violet and green vines that twisted along its surface. She tugged the bead, and the bracelet responded immediately, unfurling in one graceful motion. The mat spread across the ground, its edges perfectly even, the vines from her bracelet now winding across its surface. Jade knelt beside it, her fingers brushing the material. "It's... incredible," she said, a bit quieter than usual.

Derek gripped his bracelet with his calloused hands, his brow furrowed. His was a bolder design, its threads a mix of charcoal gray and fiery orange, the bead glowing like molten steel. He gave it a firm tug, and the transformation was striking—his mat unfurled with a sharpness that matched its design, its surface bold and angular, almost like armor laid out before him. "Cool!"

Frank, observing from under his colorful scarf by the stream, poked his head out and tilted it at the mats, his ears perked. He let out a soft whine as if asking, *Where's mine?*

Ember laughed. "Maybe next time, Frank," she said, adjusting her mat as she rose to her feet.

The three of them took their places, the clearing now transformed into a small sanctuary. The mats glowed against the mossy ground, their edges seeming to blend into the natural world. Ember stepped to the front, her posture steady and commanding, though there was a softness in her movements that invited calm.

"Let's start slow," she said, her voice carrying a natural authority. "We've earned it."

They moved together, their bodies falling into rhythm. The morning air cooled their skin as they stretched, the mats beneath them firm yet yielding, grounding them to the earth. Sunlight filtered through the canopy, creating halos around their silhouettes as they moved through the poses. Downward dog. Warrior. Dancer. The clearing seemed to respond, the gentle rustle of leaves matching their rhythm.

Derek groaned as he bent into a deeper stretch. "I'm sore in places I didn't even know existed," he exhaled.

Jade chuckled.

Frank stretched out nearby, resting his head on his paws but keeping a watchful eye on the group. The scarf draped around him shifted as he adjusted, the colors catching the light like stained glass.

As they transitioned into tree pose, their hands reaching upward, Ember glanced at the others. Their focus was steady, their breaths synchronized, and for a brief moment, the weight of their journey seemed to lift. They weren't just surviving—they were grounding themselves, finding strength in the simplicity of the practice.

When they finished, Ember guided them into a final bow, their hands pressed together in silent gratitude. One by one, their mats responded, curling back into their original forms, the threads weaving together seamlessly as they returned to bracelets.

Jade rolled her wrist, examining hers. "It feels personal," she said to herself.

Wherever you go, you are never alone. Ember recalled Joy's words. *They carry the connection of this community.* Ember slid hers back on. She felt it against her skin, a tangible reminder of Joy's wisdom.

Derek knelt by the stream, splashing water onto his face before taking a long drink. He glanced back at Ember and Jade, his expression lighter than it had been in days. "Alright," he said, adjusting his sword and brushing dirt from his knees. "Let's get moving."

Frank perked up and gave a good shake. Ember looked at the trail, winding into the forest ahead, and felt a flicker of anticipation. This wasn't just the next leg of their journey—it was a step closer to the unknown, the place where answers waited.

With their bracelets secure and their minds focused, they stepped back on the trail, the morning light guiding their path.

Frank trotted slightly ahead, his nose low to the ground, sniffing at the dirt and roots with focused curiosity. Derek walked with renewed purpose, his sword strapped firmly at his side, his jaw tight. Ember adjusted her bracelet, running her thumb over its intricate threads, grounding herself with its texture.

The path twisted into a sharper incline, its edges uneven and littered with roots. The further they walked, the heavier the air seemed to grow, no longer the fresh crispness of morning but something thicker, carrying a faint, acrid undertone. Ember paused mid-step, glancing at Derek and Jade. "Do you smell that?"

Jade nodded, her expression hardening. "Smoke. And something... burnt."

Frank stopped suddenly, his body stiff as he stared ahead, his ears perked and tail motionless. Then he barked, a sharp, anxious sound that sent a chill through the group.

"Frank?" Ember was calm but wary as she moved closer to him. The dog didn't respond, his attention locked on something further up the trail, and his right paw pulled up into his chest.

And then, through the thick underbrush, Ember spotted it—an arm lying limply over the edge of the trail, pale against the dirt and moss. Her heart lurched.

"Wait," she said sharply, holding out a hand to stop Derek and Jade from moving forward. She stepped cautiously, holding her breath as more came into view: a figure sprawled on the side of the path, motionless, clothes singed and torn, dark streaks smudged across their skin.

As she drew closer, her pulse quickened. Ember recognized the sharp lines of the tailored jacket, the gold chain visible against a bruised collarbone. Her stomach dropped.

"Susan."

CHAPTER 31

HEALING CEREMONY

Dark streaks marred her pale skin.

"Susan," Ember dropped to her knees beside the woman, her hands hovering over Susan's bruised collarbone, unsure where to begin. "What happened? Susan, can you hear me?"

Susan's eyelids fluttered, but her response was faint, more breath than sound. Ember turned to Jade, her voice rising with urgency. "Help! She's barely breathing."

Jade was already moving to Susan, swift and methodical, her voice calm but firm. "She's still breathing. Pulse is weak. Exhaustion, dehydration..." Jade's hands moved to Susan's wrist, her touch deliberate. "Looks like she's fractured her wrist."

"We need to stabilize her." She reached into her pocket and pulled out the small vial of smelling salts the healer had given her at the base of the mountain.

Derek's brow furrowed. "Will it work?"

Jade uncorked the vial and waved it gently under Susan's nose. The scent of vinegar and bleach permeated the air. Frank whined and trotted away, but Susan barely reacted. Her head lolled to one side, her breaths shallow and uneven.

"It's not enough," Jade said, her frustration slipping through her controlled tone. She sat back on her heels, her hands resting on her thighs as she considered. "Let me try something else."

"What do you mean, something else?" Derek asked.

Jade's gaze flicked to him, then Ember. Her shoulders straightened as she drew a deep breath. "It's... not exactly traditional. Something my mother taught me." She hesitated, glancing at Susan, then back at her companions. "I stopped using it years ago."

Ember nodded. "Do it."

Jade exhaled and placed her hands over Susan's chest. Her eyes closed, and she murmured softly in a language neither Ember nor Derek recognized. Her voice grew steadier, rhythmic, like the hum of the earth beneath them. The forest seemed to respond, the rustle of leaves aligning with her words. A glow pulsed beneath Jade's palms, soft and golden, spreading warmth over Susan's bruised skin.

Jade's face tightened with effort as the glow flickered and grew. Ember watched, holding her breath, as Susan's breathing evened out and her expression softened from strained to peaceful.

The glow faded, and Jade sat back, wiping her brow.

Susan remained curled, unconscious.

"That's it?" Derek asked. "That's all we can do?"

Jade turned and gave Derek a piercing look with her eyebrows raised, "We?"

Derek put his hands up and stepped back.

"And, not exactly," Jade responded. "I'm not thrilled to have to show you this side of me, but here we are. Please stand back." Derek stepped back further, and Ember stood to join him.

Jade rose slowly, the flowing green fabric of her robes catching the breeze. Its embroidery shimmered as she moved, her arms stretching outward in deliberate arcs. The energy around her shifted as her movements transformed into a dance—graceful, deliberate, yet wild with purpose. Each step felt as if it connected her to the very earth, grounding her while lifting her spirit beyond its confines.

The air thickened, vibrant with the scent of blossoms as golden flowers sprouted around her feet, unfurling toward her like hands reaching for light. The drumbeat of Jade's rhythm seemed to pulse through the clearing, synchronizing with the earth beneath her and the glow of the setting sun.

Jade spun, her movements fluid and unrestrained. Her body hovered, defying gravity as her dance became untethered from the ground. The golden embroidery of her robes gleamed the color of molten lava as the flowers bloomed in abundance. Above her, spheres of light formed, hovering between her outstretched palms.

A groan from Susan pierced the air, grounding Jade's ethereal movements. She floated downward, the light in her hands growing more focused. Jade knelt beside Susan and placed one hand gently on her chest and the other against her forehead. Her breaths deepened, and her body stilled as she channeled her energy into Susan.

Susan cried out, her back arching as energy coursed through her. Her eyes flew open, wide and unfocused, wild with fear. For a moment, Jade hesitated, a flicker of doubt crossing her face. But the glow in her hands pulsed brighter, steady and certain. The whispers of encouragement that had guided her before filled her mind once more.

"Stay with me," Jade said, her voice a steady current.

The color began to return to Susan's cheeks, the flush of life replacing the pallor of pain. Her body relaxed, her breathing evened, and the tension that had gripped her frame released. The golden light around Jade faded, and the flowers at her feet closed gently, and began retreating into the earth as if their purpose had been fulfilled.

Jade sat back, her hands dropping to her lap as she exhaled. Sweat glistened at her temples, and her shoulders sagged with the effort she had poured into the moment. "She's stabilized," Jade said with relief but also exhaustion.

Susan blinked, her gaze clearing as it settled on Jade. "What... happened?" she rasped.

"You came back to us," Jade said, brushing a loose strand of hair from Susan's face. For a moment, there was only quiet between them.

Jade reached for Susan's hand. "You're okay now," she said, her Peruvian accent slipping through, softening her words. "It will take time, but your body knows how to heal. You're stronger than you feel right now."

Susan's lips trembled as she nodded. "I thought... I wasn't going to make it this time."

"You made it because of her," Derek said, stepping closer, his gaze fixed on Jade.

"Thank you," Susan nodded at Jade.

"I admit, I'm surprised to see you here, Susan. What were you doing?" Ember asked.

Susan chuckled. "I bet you are, Ember. But I've been coming to Resonance for years. I battle burnout from the constant pressure of my career, long hours, and no real recovery. After rolling my eyes at anything woo-woo for as long as I can remember, I finally turned to meditation and breathwork when I heard CEO after CEO talking about the benefits. I got on board and, one day, I ended up here."

"Really? Huh. I've never seen you here before." Derek looked Susan over with suspicion.

"Yes, while I'm open to these practices given the health outcomes it's delivered, I'm still not one to hang with the woo-woos." Susan explained. "No offense." she added, glancing at Jade and Derek. "So when I arrive at the base with the other Breathers, I head out to hike, explore, clear my head."

She paused, her voice tightening.

"That's what I was doing, or what I thought I was doing, before I collapsed. I thought it was the altitude, maybe dehydration. But now..." Her eyes flicked to Ember. "Now I wonder if it was Resonance reflecting what was already happening to me on the outside. The burnout. The pushing. I didn't realize how close I was to breaking." She exhaled, her composure cracking. "I think this time... it caught up with me in both worlds."

"Ya well, that woo-woo stuff just saved you again," Derek clarified, in Jade's defense.

"It sure did. Jade, could you share—what was that?" Ember asked.

Jade looked at the group, her brow furrowing as if weighing how much to share. "It's something my mother taught me," she said after a pause, her voice measured.

"What exactly did you do?" Derek pressed.

Jade stood, brushing her hands on the sides of her robes. She looked away for a moment, as if searching for the right place to begin. "I grew up in a small village in the Peruvian highlands," she said, her voice soft but unwavering. "My family has always been healers. My mother, my aunts, even my grandmother. They practiced rituals that blended ancient traditions with a deep reverence for nature and the spirits of the earth."

Her gaze shifted to the golden blossoms now almost faded into the ground. "Back home, healing wasn't just about the body. It was about balance—spirit, mind, and heart. My mother would say the earth always gives us what we need if we listen."

Derek's expression softened, but his curiosity remained. "And the... floating? The spheres of light in your hands? That was incredible. That's not just listening."

Jade smiled. "That part... it's hard to explain. It's the energy we carry. The rituals I learned as a child were about connecting to that energy, to something greater than ourselves. I used to think it was... magic, maybe. But as I got older, I realized it's not magic. It's trust. Trust in what we can't see but know is there."

She hesitated, her gaze flickering between Derek and Ember. "When I was fifteen, my parents sent me to the U.S. for better opportunities. I loved science—the logic, the precision. It felt like the perfect way to blend my love of healing with something practical. I wanted to become a neurosurgeon, to understand the brain and how it connects everything we are."

"And you did it," Ember said, encouraging her to continue.

Jade nodded. "I did. But in the process, I let go of everything my mother had taught me. In the U.S., people didn't understand my beliefs. They'd laugh at me for talking about the spirits of the earth or call me superstitious. I buried that part of myself, thinking I had to choose between being a healer and being taken seriously."

She glanced down at her hands, flexing her fingers as if remembering the energy she had channeled moments ago. "It wasn't until I came here, to Resonance, that I realized I didn't have to choose. Both parts of me—science and tradition—they belong together. My mother's rituals weren't something to outgrow. They were the foundation of everything I am."

Derek crossed his arms, his expression thoughtful. "So, you've spent years running from what makes you... you."

Jade's eyes met his, steady and resolute. "Yes, I guess I have."

The silence that followed was heavy with understanding. Ember placed a hand on Jade's shoulder. "You saved her," she said simply. "You're a healer, Jade. In every sense of the word."

"I think my mother would agree with you."

Frank barked, breaking the moment, and nudged against Derek's leg. The group exchanged smiles as the tension eased.

The breeze swept through the clearing, carrying with it the scent of blossoms and earth. It felt, for a moment, as though the world had paused to acknowledge Jade's journey—and her return to herself.

Susan shifted, coming up onto her elbows. "There's something... you need to know about *your* parents, Ember." She said with urgency.

Ember froze, her heart pounding as she leaned closer. "What is it?"

Susan's expression filled with pain and, as she looked into Ember's eyes, a flicker of defiance.

"It was Dunn, Ember. Dunn killed them."

CHAPTER 32

CONVERSATION WITH SUSAN

"What do you mean Dunn killed my parents?" Susan flinched, her fingers brushing against the bruises on her arm as if the pain could ground her. She didn't meet Ember's eyes. "I mean exactly that. It wasn't an accident, Ember. He planned it."

The words struck like a physical blow, stealing Ember's breath. Her pulse raced as her mind replayed every moment she had ever spent questioning their deaths. The car crash, the vague details, the veiled conversations at the funeral. It all swirled together, more vivid now.

"Why?" Ember demanded, her fists clenching. "What could he possibly gain from killing them?"

Susan's voice faltered. "Control. Your parents were a threat to him, Ember. Your mother especially. She'd come too close to undoing everything he'd built."

Thunder rolled across the sky, low and ominous, a prelude to the rain that began to patter. The air thickened with the earthy scent of wet soil and bark, the rain creating ripples in the small pools forming around them.

Ember knelt beside Susan, her voice cutting through the steady rhythm of the rain. "Undoing what? What was she trying to do?"

Susan hesitated, her gaze dropping to the muddy ground. "Partly, undoing a mistake that she made. Your mother, Ember, she thought she could save Dunn." she said quietly.

"Save Dunn? I don't understand."

"Your mother was here, too, Ember. Here, in Resonance."

"Yes, I know that part. And she was trying to restore light to everyone here. Skip forward, Susan. Why would my mother be trying to *save* Dunn?"

"Your mother and Dunn started their disaster relief business together years ago. Back then, it was all about doing good— using cutting-edge surveillance technology to save lives. But things changed. They took on investors, and the constant pressure pushed Dunn over the edge. He started taking shortcuts, exploiting his employees, and losing sight of the original mission."

Susan hesitated before continuing. "Your mother... she knew a different Dunn once. The one with a good heart. She thought if she could remind him of the man he used to be, he might find his way back. That's why she brought him here—to Resonance."

"She brought Dunn to Resonance?" Jade interjected.

Ember sat back on her heels. Silent. Shocked.

"Yes," Susan said, barely above a whisper, and then looked up to meet Jade's eyes. "She believed Resonance would remind him of his original values, the man he used to be before he was consumed by greed and power. She never suspected that he would use it for his own gain."

She turned to Ember, "Your mother... she had this unshakable faith in people.

"When Dunn discovered Resonance, he didn't see a sanctuary—he saw an opportunity for power." Susan drew a shaky breath before continuing. "The Breathers, the ones who came here for light and renewal, weren't allies to him. They were obstacles. He realized that if he could suppress their light, he could control them—not just here, but in the real world. It gave him a way to manipulate his workforce, making them work harder, longer, without questioning anything."

She glanced at Ember. "At first, his plans hit a snag. When he found the Prism and tried to take control, Resonance itself rejected him. I can only assume it sensed his corrupted intentions. He couldn't get back here—at least, not at first."

Susan's expression darkened, her hands clutching the damp moss beneath her. "But Dunn... he's nothing if not relentless. During a particularly dangerous hurricane rescue mission, he accidentally found his way back. That's when he realized something—a near-death experience could crack open the door to Resonance. The sheer force of wanting to live was enough to pull him through."

Her voice grew sharper as she spoke, the words spilling out like they had been locked inside her for too long. "Once he figured that out, he started using it as a hack. He didn't just return alone—he brought his henchmen, his so-called Watchmen.

Together, they caged and encased the Prism, coated its surface in black, and twisted its purpose. Instead of reflecting light, it trapped it. Dunn turned Resonance into a tool for his own gain."

She fell silent, the rain now falling harder, soaking through their clothes. Ember clenched her fists, her knuckles pale as the weight of Susan's words sank in.

"And your mother, Ember, she got too close to unraveling all of this. So, Dunn orchestrated their deaths, framing them as a tragic accident."

Ember's jaw tightened, the ache in her chest spreading to her limbs. "How? How did he do it?"

Susan swallowed hard. "It wasn't just him. Dunn doesn't dirty his hands unless he has to. He used his Watchmen, his loyal followers. They orchestrated the crash, made it look like an accident. And then… they made sure no one asked questions."

Ember's eyes narrowed. "How do you know all this?"

Susan didn't answer.

"You were his lawyer," Ember pressed. "If any of this is true, sharing it with me could get you disbarred."

Susan lifted her brows and gave a tired smile. "I wasn't aware the Massachusetts Board of Bar Overseers had jurisdiction in Resonance."

The corner of Ember's mouth twitched—but the weight of Susan's words came crashing down again.

A cold, bitter silence fell over the group.

Ember's hands trembled as she fought to steady herself. "And my father?" she asked, her voice raw. "You've said nothing about him. How was he involved?"

Susan hesitated, her gaze to the ground. "He wasn't as… involved. James had grown distant, buried himself in his work. He didn't believe in Resonance the way your mother did. But he loved her, and when he realized how far Dunn would go, he tried to stop him too."

Tears pricked Ember's eyes. Her parents' lives had been taken, their light extinguished, and for what? Dunn's greed? His insatiable hunger for power?

"Why didn't you tell me this before?" Ember asked, rain now streaking down her cheeks.

Susan's face twisted with something between guilt and defiance. "Because I thought I could protect you. I thought if you stayed on Dunn's good side, you'd be safe."

Ember stood, the rain plastering her hair to her face, her body trembling with barely contained rage. "Safe?" she spat. "You thought keeping me in the dark would protect me? He killed my parents, Susan. He destroyed my family. And you want me to play nice?"

Susan pushed herself up against a rock, her voice rising in desperation. "You don't understand, Ember. He's stronger than you think. If you go after him, you'll end up just like them."

Ember moved closer, her eyes blazing. "I'm not my parents. I won't make the same mistakes."

Susan shook her head, her expression pleading. "You can't defeat him, Ember. He knows you're coming. He's prepared for you."

Ember considered this information. Her demeanor shifted; emotions now locked away behind a practiced calm. She stepped fully into attorney mode: precise, analytical, and unyielding. This wasn't the time for raw emotion or reckless action. The days of walking blindly into the unknown were over. Ember's mind focused with laser clarity—she would extract every piece of information Susan had and use it to craft a plan. Preparation was her weapon now.

Ember's voice broke through the rain, "Why didn't my mother make it, Susan?"

Susan hesitated, brushing wet strands of hair from her face. "She would have—she was so close—but she was alone. Her heart was broken, Ember. Your father... he was too far gone. Stuck in the grind for so long, he couldn't get back to Resonance. He'd built this... shell around himself. A corporate exoskeleton, so rigid nothing could break through."

Ember's jaw tightened as she leaned closer. "So, she was close to defeating Dunn? Close to freeing the Prism?"

Susan nodded slowly, her voice tinged with regret. "Yes. And that's why Dunn had them killed. Cynthia, your mother, had gotten too close, and he wasn't willing to take any chances. He couldn't risk her succeeding. He has only weeks left until a massive payout from his private equity deal—his light at the end of the tunnel. He needs everyone working harder than ever, nose to the grindstone, no time for joy or freedom. If anyone threatens that, Ember, he eliminates them. No hesitation."

Ember's breath quickened as the weight of Susan's words pressed down on her. "How was she going to do it? How was my mother planning to defeat him?"

Susan met Ember's gaze, her voice somber. "With her light, Ember. That's all it takes. She just needed to get close enough to the Prism."

Ember frowned, her frustration bleeding through. "If he was that desperate to stop her, why hasn't he just killed me too?"

Susan's shoulders sagged as she sighed. "Because Cynthia was going to sacrifice herself to destroy him. Dunn's entire hold on Resonance is rooted in exploiting others for his gain. An act of pure selflessness, offering her light not for power but to free others, would've shattered the cage he built around the Prism. He knew she'd make that choice, so he made it for her. As for you, Ember... you weren't a threat to him back then. But now? Now you are."

Ember's chest tightened. "So, that's what's waiting for me? I'll have to... sacrifice myself?"

A heavy silence lingered before Derek, who had been quietly watching, finally spoke. "What about me?" His voice was low. "Does that mean it's waiting for me too?" For a fleeting moment, he wished he could let go of his light, avoid the responsibility it carried.

Susan shook her head, her expression clouded with uncertainty. "I don't know. None of us do. It's never been done before."

Ember turned away, her thoughts spiraling. Self-sacrifice? Could that really be the cost of restoring Resonance? She couldn't accept it—not yet. There had to be another way. A smarter way. She pressed her lips into a thin line, unwilling to believe that the only path forward was the one her mother had taken.

The rain fell harder, but Ember straightened, the fire in her eyes refusing to dim. Whatever lay ahead, she wasn't going to let fear dictate her next move. She would face Dunn, and she would win—on her terms.

Susan's voice was strained, her eyes shadowed with urgency. "Time is short, Ember. Don't risk it. Just go home. Please."

Ember held Susan's gaze for a long moment, her expression unreadable. Finally, she nodded. "You're right. We'll sleep here tonight and head back to the base in the morning."

Relief softened Susan's tense features, and she exhaled. "Good. That's the smartest thing you can do right now."

Derek frowned, his frustration evident. "We're retreating?"

Ember raised her hand, silencing him with a pointed look and a small, knowing smile that only he could see. Derek sighed, stepping back and muttering under his breath, but he said nothing more.

Jade crossed her arms and looked to Susan. "And you? What are you going to do now?"

Susan hesitated before glancing toward a break in the trees. "There's a trail nearby. It leads to a vista—a place I've always loved. I'll go there to recover and clear my head."

"Take care of yourself, Ember." The group watched as Susan limped away, her figure disappearing into the mist.

Once she was gone, Derek turned to Ember. "We're not actually going back, are we?"

Ember shook her head, her expression hardening. "No. We're going to make a plan."

As she spoke, the air shifted. A green light flashed across the valley, brilliant and sharp, cutting through the mist like a jagged blade. The pulse was cold and clinical, unnatural in its precision.

Ember whipped around towards the flash. "What was that?"

Derek frowned, his grip tightening on his sword. "That's not the Prism, is it?"

"No," Ember said, her voice hard. "That's Dunn."

The green light pulsed again, sending ripples through the air that rattled their bones. Frank barked, his fur bristling as he lowered himself to the ground. The ridge beneath them trembled, small rocks tumbling into the abyss below.

"What's he doing?" Jade stammered.

Ember's jaw clenched as her mind raced. The flashes felt deliberate, a signal—not of preparation, but of control. "He knows we're coming," she said. "And he's making sure we know it, too."

Jade took a step closer to Ember. "This isn't just a warning. He's baiting us."

Ember nodded, her gaze narrowing. "Good. That means he's afraid."

The green light flared one last time, brighter and more intense, before the valley fell silent.

The group exchanged a look, each silently steeling themselves. Frank nudged Ember's leg.

As they began to move again, the path sloping higher and narrower, Ember felt a flicker of clarity through the chaos. This wasn't just a fight against Dunn—it was a reckoning. A test. Her true challenge wouldn't be brute force or even strategy. It would be outthinking him, unraveling the lies that bound Resonance to his control, and wielding the truth like a weapon.

CHAPTER 33

TAKE SHELTER

The storm intensified, rain drumming on the rocky outcrop where Ember, Derek, Jade, and Frank found refuge. They huddled just inside the mouth of a cave, the downpour forming a watery curtain that blurred their view of the valley and distant peaks. Occasional lightning flashes illuminated the landscape, casting shadows across their faces.

"We can't do it alone, but we have to try," Derek said, his eyes fixed on the expanse beyond the cave.

Ember began taking inventory, her voice clear above the storm. "What advantages do we have? We have my light, and yours now, Derek." She turned to Jade and noticed a distant look on her face. "What's wrong, Jade?"

Jade exhaled, and her shoulders dropped. "Honestly? I thought after helping Susan I'd finally have my light. Derek faced his fear, and I faced something deeply personal, too. I thought maybe it would awaken within me." Her voice softened. "Now I'm conflicted—both of you are intact, you have it, and you are willing to put that at risk. You are sacrificing so much. What if, in the end, you restore it and I'm the only one with light left?"

"You're overthinking, Jade" Derek cut in. "Come here." He placed his hand on the damp stone floor beside him. "Ground yourself. Everything is okay. We'll figure it out."

Jade hesitated, then joined him, her breathing steadying as she touched the earth.

A silence settled over them, interrupted only by the rain and Frank's panting. Ember paced, inventorying their strengths. "We have your sword, Derek, and Jade's salts. And we have… yoga mats?" She raised an eyebrow, her voice tinged with amusement. They shared a small, welcome laugh.

Frank barked, drawing their attention. Ember laughed. "And of course, we have you, Frank."

"Dunn's greatest weapon is getting inside people's heads," Derek said, leaning forward. "We have to stay mentally strong."

"Right," Ember agreed. "We must stay open to each other, true to who we are, but find a way to block him. We can't let him distract us. But how do we stay open and yet protect ourselves from him at the same time?"

Frank's tail wagged, his eyes bright even in the gloom.

"Anger and determination," Ember continued, her voice steady now. "That's what we have most of all. Dunn killed my parents. We need to channel that anger, use it to stay focused. He'll expect us eventually, but Susan said we've made it faster than he anticipated. We still have surprise."

Jade folded her arms, her expression unreadable. "Even with that," she began, "say we can take him by surprise and get to the Prism. Then what? How do we open the cage?"

Derek exhaled, his fingers flexing around the hilt of his sword. The last time he had tried—when Sirenna had taunted him—nothing had happened. Just a hollow failure that had sunk into his bones. But that was before.

Now, he had his light.

"I have an idea," he said, stepping away from the group and into the storm. Rain lashed against his skin, but he barely felt it. His focus locked on a massive boulder jutting from the earth, slick with water and worn by time.

The wind howled through the valley as he raised the sword, the jagged crystal catching the flashes of lightning above. His breath steadied, his heartbeat aligning with the steady thrum of power inside him. This time, he *knew*.

With a swift, forceful arc, he brought the sword down.

Crack!

The crystal met stone—and the boulder erupted in an explosion of blinding brilliance. Shards of rock fractured outward, but instead of falling as heavy debris, they splintered into streaks of glittering light. Flashes of molten gold and deep sapphire flared against the storm-dark sky, swirling with bursts of violet and silver. The air vibrated with the impact, sending waves of iridescent color rippling outward, casting fleeting rainbows through the falling rain. A deep, resonant hum pulsed from the sword, as if it had awakened fully for the first time.

Derek stood amidst the aftermath, his chest rising and falling, the blade still glowing in his grasp. He turned to the others.

Jade's mouth parted, stunned. Ember stepped forward, the last flickers of refracted light reflected in her eyes.

"Looks like it works," Derek said, his voice rough with something that wasn't quite relief, wasn't quite triumph—but something raw.

Jade and Ember stood frozen, their breath stolen by the sight before them. The moment Derek's sword struck the boulder, the world seemed to bend around it.

The boulder hadn't just cracked—it had fractured into pure brilliance. The pieces had exploded outward, glittering like a thousand miniature prisms before dissolving into the mist.

Jade exhaled, her fingers twitching as if resisting the urge to reach toward the dissipating light. "That wasn't just blunt force," she said. "That was... something more."

Ember took a step forward, her pulse thrumming in her ears. She had *felt* it—that shift, that undeniable moment of power unfurling from within Derek. This was something far greater than skill.

Derek turned toward them, his grip still firm around the hilt. He rolled his shoulders, testing the weight of the sword as if it had only now fully become his. Derek's eyes were alight with something Ember had never seen before. Not just confidence—certainty.

Frank barked, then gave a vigorous shake, sending droplets of rain and lingering flecks of light scattering into the air. The shimmer clung to his fur for a heartbeat longer before dissolving.

Ember's gaze moved between Derek and the place where the boulder had stood. "If that's what your sword can do," she said slowly, "then we have a real chance."

Derek exhaled, the last remnants of the light fading from the air around them. "Then let's go prove it."

Ember regained her composure. "Perfect," Ember said, determination settling in. "Derek, you'll open the cage. And we'll just have to trust that our light is strong enough for the rest."

"And me?" Jade asked, "What do I do?"

Ember looked at her friend steadily. "Please, Jade, strengthen us first. We need clear minds and brave hearts to avoid distraction."

"What?" Jade protested. "I'm coming!" Frank barked in solidarity.

Ember stepped closer. "This is my fight, Jade. You've already done more than enough. If we fail, we'll need you."

Jade scowled but reluctantly nodded. Derek turned to Frank, bending to the dog's level. "Frank, you're staying here to protect Jade. There's no place for a dog in battle."

Frank protested with a low whine, but Derek held his gaze. "Protect Jade."

Frank huffed, acknowledging the seriousness of his charge, and lay down next to Jade.

"Alright," Jade sighed, accepting her role. She began gathering flowers and herbs near the cave's edge, preparing herself for the ceremony, resolved despite her reluctance.

The storm hammered down, drowning out the sound of footsteps on distant trails—forces were aligning, sides were forming, and soon they'd know who stood with them and who stood against.

CHAPTER 34

WHICH SIDE AM I ON?

Susan paused on the winding trail, the twilight deepening around her. The last remnants of sunlight painted the sky in streaks of burnt orange and indigo, casting long shadows across her path. Her breath came in short, shallow bursts, and she began pacing, her boots crunching against the gravel. She tugged at her dark auburn hair, the strands whipping in the rising wind.

Her sharp cheekbones and defined jawline, so often composed and unreadable, were now tense with indecision. A deep crease formed between her brows, her striking green eyes clouded with doubt. Normally, she carried herself with effortless grace, her movements precise and deliberate, honed from years of maneuvering through corporate circles.

But here, now, she was unraveling.

"Why?" she hissed up into the darkening sky, voice raw with frustration. "Why now, why this?" The wind rustled through the trees, indifferent to her turmoil.

Ember's face flashed in her mind—strong, resolute, fiercely loyal. Susan felt an ache deep in her chest. Yet the comforts of the castle, her status, the security Dunn provided—it all loomed large, powerful, and undeniable. She pressed a trembling hand to the delicate gold chain around her neck, a subtle reminder of the world she had fought to secure for herself.

She placed a hand on her chest, feeling her heartbeat quicken. Images of Ember, Derek, and Jade flooded her mind—their unshakable resolve and the warmth of friendship she'd never expected to find. The thought sent a rush of longing through her, a flicker of something real, something she had spent so long keeping at arm's length.

But as she turned toward the castle, its golden lights glowing in the twilight, its towering silhouette a fortress of familiarity, her mind recoiled, retreating to the safety of logic, of reason. Stability was power. And power meant survival.

Her fingers curled into a fist at her side.

"Ember... I'm sorry," she whispered into the empty air, tears blurring her vision. She steadied herself, drew a deep breath, and pressed forward.

The truth was still pounding in her chest. For a moment, with Ember, Susan had felt like she was in the middle of everything she used to believe in. Doing the right thing. That was why she'd gone to law school in the first place. Not to shield men like Dunn, to protect power, but to help people. Somewhere along the way, she'd lost that. Buried it beneath ambition, long hours, and the kind of clients who paid enough to make her forget why she'd started.

She found Dunn in the grand hall, standing near a towering window, assessing the darkening landscape below. Dunn's figure was imposing; tall, with a sharp, angular face etched with lines of power and privilege. His dark suit contrasted with the shimmering gold chains encircling his wrists and neck, their glint cold and mesmerizing in the low light.

He turned, acknowledging her presence with a barely perceptible nod.

"Susan," Dunn said, his tone measured, professional. He looked her over—hair dripping, clothes soaked through, one hand cradling her wrist. "You look like hell," he said with disdain. "Where have you been? What were you doing out there, anyway?"

She stiffened, slipping the mask back on. "Checking the perimeter. Assessing risks—doing my job. You know me, NP, I don't like surprises. Especially ones that pose threats to you."

This was the role. This was who she had to be. She'd spent years building her reputation, her wealth, her life—and it was all still tethered to him. To this.

He studied her, his eyes searching. "And did you find what you were looking for?"

"Yes," Susan replied, holding his gaze. "Ember is here. With others. She's strong—stronger than expected. She says she's heading back down to base, but I don't believe her."

Dunn paused, eyes narrowed. "You're certain there's a genuine threat?"

"I am," she said, the words bitter on her tongue. "You should assemble the Watchmen. Just in case."

Dunn nodded. "Thank you, Susan. Hector!" His voice rang with authority, and Hector appeared. Hector was weathered, his frame bent, wrinkles carved into his bulbous features from years of toil.

"Mobilize all Watchmen," Dunn ordered. "Inform Sirenna that she'll have company moving through her palace tonight."

Hector nodded, his face impassive, and vanished to execute his orders.

Dunn walked past Susan, pausing briefly, the golden chain around his wrist clinking as he touched her shoulder in acknowledgment. "Good work, Susan. I won't forget it." He paused, then added, "I'll let Roland know where things stand."

As Dunn's footsteps faded into the echoing hall, Susan's knees weakened. Her hand reached for the ornate table, desperate for something solid. Her earlier resolve crumbled, giving way to the familiar emptiness. The hollow comfort of expensive choices.

She closed her eyes.

This was the cost of staying afloat. Of keeping the penthouse and the corner office and the illusion of control.

She had tried—for one brief moment—to break free.

But the gold always pulled her back in.

A chill crept up her spine. There was no turning back now.

CHAPTER 35

STRENGTH

The rain had finally stopped, leaving behind droplets that glittered like jewels across the lush foliage surrounding the cave. Jade moved to the cave's edge beside Frank, breathing and centering herself. The murmur of the forest grew softer. Ember and Derek stood quietly, holding steady through the anticipation and uncertainty of the moment. Frank sat, alert and watchful, his ears perked.

Jade raised her hands, palms open to the sky. A soft glow ignited at her fingertips, tendrils of golden energy rising like smoke, swirling around her wrists. Her voice was calm, infused with strength.

"Feel the earth beneath you," she began, eyes closed. "Let it ground your resolve."

She moved fluidly, stepping into a slow, deliberate dance, each gesture carrying intention and grace. Golden energy began to weave around her, delicate strands intertwining into glowing symbols that floated in the air, suspended like liquid starlight. Her movements gained momentum, a rhythmic pulse echoing through the clearing.

The ground beneath their feet vibrated, resonating with her movements. Ribbons of energy flowed outward, encircling Ember and Derek, weaving patterns of protection and power. Ember felt a surge within her, an electric warmth flooding her senses. Derek's hand found its way to grip his crystal sword.

"Remember," Jade's voice deepened, resonating with conviction, "the power you hold is in your openness, your heart. But you must guard it fiercely against distraction and fear. Stay open but let nothing break your focus."

Her movements gained momentum, building into a rhythmic pulse that echoed through the clearing. With each turn, the golden symbols grew larger, blazing with a vibrant intensity, connecting and encircling Ember and Derek in a powerful web of protection and purpose.

"You go to confront not just Dunn, but the shadows he commands," Jade's voice boomed, unwavering. "They will try to trap you, to make you forget. Remember who you are, remember this strength."

With a final sweep of her arms, Jade sent the radiant symbols surging toward Ember and Derek. The symbols dissolved into their chests, a surge of energy rushing through Ember. Beside her, Derek squared his shoulders.

Jade lowered her arms, the glow receding slowly into the earth. Ember stood taller, her spirit unshakable. Derek's eyes shone bright with resolve.

"Trust yourselves," Jade said firmly. "You have everything you need. Mind, heart, and spirit—you are ready."

Ember nodded, determined. Without a word, they turned toward the opening of the cave and set out for the trail, continuing their ascent with newfound purpose.

•◆•

Jade stood at the cave's edge beside Frank, watching as Ember and Derek disappeared up the trail. She raised a hand in farewell, eyes steady. Jade took another deep breath, the energy of the ceremony still humming within her, and moved back into the shelter of the cave, Frank close by her side.

"Now," Jade whispered, and placed her hand on Frank's head as she sat. "We wait."

CHAPTER 36

UP

The peak rose sharp and imposing ahead of them, silhouetted against the fading amber sky. Ember paused, breathing heavily, the crisp mountain air biting at her lungs as she adjusted her footing on the uneven trail. Derek stopped beside her, his crystal sword gleaming in the waning daylight.

From here, Ember could see their destination clearly: at the summit, a massive golden cage loomed, its bars thick and unyielding. But it was the Prism inside that caught her attention, ensnared beneath a suffocating layer of black—a slick, unnatural coating that swallowed the light instead of reflecting it. Yet beneath the darkness, the Prism still fought, glimmers of color spiraling wildly in frantic bursts, flickering like dying embers desperate to ignite once more.

Her jaw tightened.

"We're almost there," Derek said, eyes locked ahead. He adjusted his grip on the sword, the facets casting specks of rainbow across his fingers.

"It's too easy," Ember murmured, squinting toward the unguarded cage. "Why isn't he protecting it?"

Derek shrugged. "Maybe he doesn't think he needs to."

Ember looked at him, her gaze fierce. "Well, he's about to find out he's wrong."

Derek nodded. They locked eyes for a moment, a quiet acknowledgment passing between them. Neither said it aloud, but they both knew—no matter what came next, neither would stop until Dunn's power was broken.

Ember moved first, her boots sinking into the damp moss. Derek followed close, eyes trained ahead.

As they climbed, their pace slowed. The incline grew sharper, the path littered with loose stones and hidden roots. Derek stumbled, catching himself against a jagged rock with a grunt of annoyance. Ember offered a hand without looking back, and he took it, pulling himself up with her help.

Reaching the crest, they found a large, flat boulder, half-buried beneath overgrown ferns. Ember paused, breathing heavily. "This looks like a good place to stop and think this through."

Derek nodded, wiping sweat from his brow, and they ducked behind the boulder, dropping into a crouch.

Ember peered around the stone, eyes narrowing at the cage still standing suspiciously unguarded. "So, the cage," she whispered, her voice tight with tension, "is there any chance your sword won't work? Could Dunn have reinforced it?"

Derek turned the crystal sword in his hands, examining it thoughtfully. "If this sword resonates with my heart, it should have enough power to break the cage," he reasoned. "And if it doesn't, well…" He trailed off, his mouth quirking into a sardonic half-smile. "Then we'll have bigger problems."

Ember's eyes narrowed. "We only get one chance at this. Dunn won't give us another. It's now or never," she whispered, her voice quiet but unwavering. "He took my parents from me. I refuse to let him take anything else."

Derek met her gaze. "Then let's finish this."

They stood, stepping cautiously from their hiding place. Ember took one final steadying breath, preparing herself for whatever came next. But before they could take another step forward, the quiet was shattered by a distant, mechanical hum that grew rapidly louder, slicing through the stillness.

"Drone," Derek spat, recognition flooding his face. He shifted defensively, sword raised. "Surveillance. Dunn's tech."

•◆•

A sleek, metallic shape streaked toward them, fast and menacing. Before Derek could react, a black beam shot out, striking him directly in the temple. He staggered, bracing for pain, but felt none. Instead, his mind flooded with insidious voices.

You're nothing. The whispers taunted. *Insignificant. Unworthy.*

•◆•

"Derek!" Ember cried out, her voice sharp with panic. She grabbed his shoulders, shaking him hard. His eyes were glazed, vacant. "Derek, fight it!"

He blinked slowly. His breathing quickened, pupils dilating in panic. "This is what happened to the Wanderers," he gasped, voice shaking. "Ember, they're shooting distraction. They're getting inside our heads."

"Focus on me," Ember urged. "We've got this. We know what to do."

• ◆ •

Above, inside his fortress, NP Dunn lounged casually with his executives, swirling a cocktail. Hector burst in. "Dunn. They're near the Prism."

"WHAT?" Dunn roared, his glass shattered in his fist. "It's too soon. Deploy every drone we've got. Get everyone to the observation deck—now!"

• ◆ •

From above, a hail of drones converged on Ember and Derek, their sleek black forms slicing the sky. The air pulsed with the high-pitched whine of their engines, and then, all at once, they started firing.

Black smoky tendrils erupted from their undersides, striking like vipers. They moved fast—erratic, twisting through the air before lashing out with terrifying precision.

Derek ducked as one snapped past his head. Another shot toward Ember's chest. She pivoted, barely dodging, but the next tendril struck her forearm and didn't bounce off—it sank in.

A chilling sensation shot through her veins, not cold, not hot—something other, something wrong. The tendril's blackness curled beneath her skin like ink dissolving in water.

Then, the whispers began.

You're losing time, Ember. You've already failed. Just stop.

The voice was hers, but not hers. Warped, stretched. A thought that felt like her own but carried an edge of something foreign.

She ripped her arm free with a sharp gasp, the tendril tearing away like smoke retreating from flame. But its mark lingered— the whisper still echoed in her mind, threading through her thoughts like a splinter she couldn't pull out.

• ◆ •

A tendril struck Derek's back, sinking deep. His steps faltered.

Why are you fighting, Derek? You could never matter enough to win.

His vision blurred. The storm, the Prism, even Ember beside him—it all felt suddenly distant, like a memory he wasn't sure was real.

"Derek, shake it off!" Ember's voice cut through the haze, sharp, real. "It's NOT YOU. It's THEM."

Derek gasped, his breath coming fast and shallow. He forced himself to move, to push through the fog clawing at his mind.

• ◆ •

"We have to go," Ember panted.

You can't win. You never could.

Her knees buckled. The Prism blurred in her vision. The pull to surrender was overwhelming, to just stop and let the thoughts drown her.

No.

She clenched her fists, forcing herself to breathe. She gritted her teeth and pushed back, clawing her way to the surface of her own mind. She would not fall.

Derek shook his head violently, fighting against the sickly tendrils wrapping around his thoughts. His sword pulsed in his grip, flickering like a heart.

Focus. Focus. Focus on what's real.

Another shot skimmed past, but this time, Derek was ready. He turned the blade in a sharp arc, catching the next blast on its crystal edge. The black smoke shattered into iridescent light, dissipating harmlessly.

Ember met his eyes. They didn't need to speak. They would reach the Prism.

Together, they ran.

Dunn emerged onto his observation balcony, incredulous and furious. "Why aren't the drones working?" he shouted. "They should be forgetting by now! That damn light can't protect them forever!"

Below, Derek and Ember finally reached the golden cage. Ember's heart racing. Derek gripped his sword tightly, drawing it back, ready to strike.

Ember locked eyes with Dunn, who glared down at her, teeth gritted in fury. "Do it, Derek," she urged.

Derek swung with all the strength of his heart and the power of the crystal sword—brilliant, fierce, confident. Ember braced for an explosive breakthrough. Instead, the sword bounced off with a hollow, dull clang. Ember's eyes widened in shock, looking to Derek desperately.

He swung again.

Clang.

Above them, Dunn erupted into laughter, harsh and mocking. He leaned over the railing, voice dripping with contempt. "You actually thought you could restore the Prism? Ha! You're just like your parents, Ember—always ambitious, never enough. Never quite smart enough."

Before Ember could respond, Dunn flicked his wrist, launching a golden chain from above. It wrapped around Ember's wrist, searing her skin, leaving a permanent brand. Pain jolted through her, momentarily blinding.

More drones descended rapidly, firing relentlessly. Derek seized Ember's arm, urgency in his voice, "Ember, we have to go!"

"No, we can't—" she protested weakly, tugging at the chain.

"Now, Ember!" Derek shouted, pulling her from the cage. They bolted down the trail, stumbling blindly through blasts and debris, pursued by the swarm. Ember's legs burned and her lungs felt about to collapse.

Finally, the drones began to fall away, leaving them panting and bruised on the edge of safety. Ember collapsed against a fallen tree, gasping, pain radiating from the golden chain seared around her wrist.

Derek knelt beside her. Ember stared at the chain, skin blistered beneath the intricate metal, searing as if Dunn himself gripped her wrist. The humiliation of defeat burned deeper than the pain.

Their eyes met, acknowledging silently what neither wished to say aloud. They had underestimated Dunn, their bravado shattered.

"We underestimated him," Derek finally admitted.

Ember took a deep, ragged breath, "But he underestimated us, too."

In the darkening forest, their shared look was fierce, unspoken determination flowing between them. They'd lost this battle, but the war was far from over.

And Ember would not make the same mistake twice.

CHAPTER 37

CHAINED

Her eyelids fluttered, the blurred outlines of trees and shadows swirling together. Everything felt off—too light, too unsteady. But there was movement. A steady rhythm beneath her. A firm grip holding her.

Derek's breathing thrummed in her ear, even but strained.

Ember blinked, forcing focus. He was carrying her.

Her body was slung in his arms, his grip solid under her knees and back, muscles tensed as he maneuvered carefully over the uneven ground.

"Derek," she rasped, her throat dry. "What—what happened?"

"You went down. One second we were walking and talking and the next, I turn back and you're crumpled on the trail."

She pushed against his chest, trying to sit up. "Put me down. I can walk."

"Not yet."

"Derek."

"You weren't moving, Ember." His voice was calm but clipped, a layer of something underneath—something close to anger, but not quite.

She swallowed, pressing a hand to her temple. She could still feel the smoke curling around her head, its weight pressing in, the whispers of her own voice telling her to stop, to let go.

But she hadn't.

And she wasn't about to be carried like she had.

With more force, she shoved against his chest. "I said put me down."

Derek exhaled through his nose but relented, lowering her to the ground.

Frank's panicked bark pierced through the air, and Ember felt a burst of relief. Jade rushed out from the shadows of the cave, eyes wide with worry.

"What happened?" Jade's voice trembled, betraying a rare vulnerability.

Frank pressed his cold nose urgently into Ember's palm, whining softly as she scratched behind his ears, seeking comfort in the familiar roughness of his fur.

"It didn't work," Derek's voice cracked as he lowered himself beside her, wiping his brow with a shaking hand. "We were close, but…"

"Come tell me. Come in. Rest. I'll make you some tea." Jade hurried them into the safety of the cave.

Jade gathered small bundles of dried herbs from her supplies. She quickly crushed them onto a broad, concave leaf she'd found earlier, pouring water she'd collected from a nearby stream into it. She stirred the mixture briskly with a slender twig, then carefully handed the makeshift cup first to Ember, her eyes sharp with concern.

"Drink this," Jade insisted. Ember took the leaf cup with unsteady hands, inhaling deeply.

Derek took his turn, sipping from the leaf, tension still evident in his posture. Jade's gaze landed on Ember's wrist, and her eyes narrowed.

"What is that?" she asked, pointing.

Ember looked down, dread pooling in her stomach. A gold chain, intricate and cruelly beautiful, encircled her wrist, shimmering. The skin beneath it burned like fire.

"Dunn shot it at me," Ember said. "It roped around my wrist. I don't know what it means, but it hurts."

The three sat in silence, with Frank shifting anxiously at Ember's feet. Jade finally broke the quiet, her voice practical yet gentle. "We regroup. We plan. And we try again."

"I'm not ready to search for the solution right now, Jade. I need a minute," Ember said, pulling herself up with effort. Derek started to rise, his shoulders tense, hands reaching out, ready to steady Ember if she wavered. But Jade laid a hand on his shoulder, shaking her head.

"Give her space," Jade whispered.

Fayra's words echoed through Ember's mind, circling, lingering. *You won't be alone.*

The words should have brought comfort, but instead, they left her unsettled. Alone in what? Who would stand with her? Who was missing? She turned the phrase over and over.

She exhaled slowly, pressing her palm against the cave wall, grounding herself in the cool stone. The words echoed again, softer now, like a whisper carried on the wind.

You won't be alone.

She closed her eyes, waiting for an answer that didn't come.

CHAPTER 38

THE WORRY STONE

Ember went out to the clearing, which stretched wide beneath
the sky, the late afternoon light casting golden fingers
through the dense forest canopy. She stood in the center,
surveying. The weight of failure still sat heavy on her chest—the
battle lost, Dunn's golden chain burned into her wrist, Derek's
sword unable to break the cage.

That heart-wrenching sound.

Clang.

She exhaled, unclasping the yoga mat bracelet from her
other wrist, the intricate threads pressing into her skin before
she unfurled it. The fabric rippled outward, unfolding into a
mat woven with gold, blue, and crimson—deep, interlaced hues
that shimmered like silk. Ember lowered herself onto the mat,
crossed her legs, and pulled the worry stone from her pocket.

She rolled it between her fingers, the smoothness grounding
her in the present. A deep breath in. A slow breath out. The
forest faded.

Darkness curled at the edges of her vision. Then—warmth.

A presence.

A woman stood before her, bathed in the soft glow of twilight. Silver-gold hair framed her face, cut short but swept back, as if shaped by the wind. Lines of wisdom softened her features, but her presence was anything but fragile. She wore a vest of deep burgundy, beads at her collar catching the light. And at the center of her chest, a golden radiance pulsed; faint at first, then brighter, glittering like the sun on the water.

Ember gasped.

"Mom?"

The world around her stilled.

She wasn't imagining it. Here she was, standing in the space between the dying sun and the rising stars.

The light in her eyes held something deeper now, something Ember had only glimpsed in fleeting childhood moments when she caught her mother looking at her like this. Like she already knew the end of a story Ember was only beginning to understand.

She smiled. "You've come far, Ember. But you're still looking in the wrong place."

Ember swallowed. "I don't understand. We tried. We fought. And we lost." She whispered, as if speaking the word too loudly might shatter the moment.

Ember's fingers curled into fists at her sides, the golden glow at her chest flickering. "I was trying to protect myself."

Her mother's gaze softened, and she reached out—not to touch Ember, but to hover her palm just above her heart, where the light pulsed beneath her skin.

"And in protecting yourself, you shut yourself away."

Ember trembled. The warmth radiating from her mother's presence wasn't just external—it was reaching inside her, uncoiling something tight and buried deep.

Tears burned at the edges of Ember's eyes. She wanted to fall into her mother's arms, to touch her, to hold onto this moment and never let go. But she didn't dare move. She was afraid if she did, her mother would vanish.

Her mother tilted her head, her smile tinged with something bittersweet. "You already know what to do, Ember. You've always known."

The truth washed over Ember.

She knew.

She had spent so much time guarding her mind against Dunn, so much time trying to outthink him, that she had closed the very thing that made her strong. Her light had never been about logic. It had never been about battle strategy.

It was about connection.

I must keep my heart open to connect with the Wanderers.

She inhaled, the glow at her chest burning brighter, steadier.

When she lifted her gaze again, her mother was fading, dissolving into the last remnants of twilight.

"No—WAIT!" Ember shouted, stepping forward, reaching out even though she knew she wouldn't feel anything.

Her mother's voice was no more than a breath against the wind.

"You are never alone."

And then, she was gone.

The words curled in Ember's chest, filling the empty spaces. A warmth lingered—not just from the vision, but something deeper, something real. She pressed a hand to her heart, feeling the rhythm of it, steady, unshaken.

Firelight flickered in the distance. The others would be waiting.

She pushed to her feet. As she did, her gaze drifted to the golden chain Dunn had burned into her wrist. The metal still pulsed, as if tethered to him.

She turned toward the trail. She knew what had to be done.

By the time she reached their makeshift camp, the fire had burned low. The air smelled of damp earth and pine, and the night stretched wide above them, streaked with the last traces of twilight.

Derek and Jade looked up as she stepped into the glow. Jade was crouched over a steaming leaf cup, while Derek ran his thumb along the edge of his sword, his expression unreadable. Shadows lingered beneath their eyes, exhaustion settling into the lines of their faces.

Ember didn't hesitate.

"We were too focused on fighting him," she said, her voice steady. "We can't just block him out—we must stay open. That's where our strength is." She met each of their gazes in turn. "We're going to the Wanderers first thing in the morning. If we can help them remember who they are, they'll break free of the cycles Dunn has trapped them in. They'll want to fight."

Jade studied her, her fingers tightening around the cup. "You really think they can come back?"

"I know they can."

Derek exhaled, rolling his shoulders before giving a nod. "Let's get some sleep, then. We need to be at full strength."

Frank circled the fire, then flopped down beside Ember, his warmth grounding her. Frank pressed his nose to her palm. She exhaled, threading her fingers through his fur.

The forest loomed beyond them.

Tomorrow, they would find the Wanderers.

Tomorrow, they would help them remember.

CHAPTER 39

THE LAST SUPPER

The mountain loomed over Resonance like a sleeping beast, its jagged cliffs swallowing the sky in darkness. The summit, carved into a fortress of stone and steel, housed the elite—those who had climbed high enough, taken enough, or proven themselves useful enough to remain. Below, the valley sprawled in shifting hues of violet and gold, the last remnants of sunset bleeding into the unnatural glow that pulsed from the Prism's cage.

But NP Dunn barely noticed the view.

He had always known he was destined to rule something greater than men. That much had been clear when he cracked the code—when he figured out how to break into Resonance, how to seize its power, how to mold it into something *useful*.

Others had stumbled in, aimless, lost in dreams and distractions. He had been the first to understand.

He had shaped the Prism's cage.

He had written the rules.

Yet tonight, he was angry.

No one had ever made it this far. And they were ahead of schedule.

The heavy doors of the mountaintop castle creaked as they shut behind him. Inside the dining room, his most trusted advisors stood waiting, the select few who had earned their seats at his table. The air was thick with burning cedar, smoke curling through the golden chandelier of interlocking chains that swayed above them. The table itself—black obsidian, polished to a mirrored finish—was set for a feast no one had touched.

This was a war room disguised in civility.

Seated at the table were five of Dunn's highest-ranking confidants, each one carefully chosen, each one indispensable in their own way. Some were loyal, some were dangerous. And the ones who Dunn valued most? They were both.

Dunn didn't sit. He placed his hands on the back of his chair, staring down at the untouched plates. He inhaled deeply, steadying his pulse, but beneath his ribcage, something seethed.

"They're ahead of schedule," he said, his voice a razor against the brittle quiet.

No one responded immediately.

Hector, seated to his left, adjusted his cufflinks. Ex-military, thick with the weight of battles won and wars lost, he had the patience of a man who had survived worse. "It's being handled," he finally said, his voice like gravel.

Dunn's fingers curled against the leather of his chair. His eyes flicked to the woman across from him—Sirenna, regal in her dark silk, her black nails tapping idly against the stem of her wine glass. Her gaze challenged Dunn.

"You assured me the Palace would hold them."

Sirenna lifted her chin, the corner of her mouth twitching. She always enjoyed these moments—watching him fray, just a little.

"And you assured me she was just a girl," she said, swirling the burgundy wine in her glass, letting the silence stretch.

Dunn exhaled sharply through his nose, his fingers pressing into the table's edge. He leveled his gaze at her, voice low and edged with impatience.

"Spare me the games, Sirenna. *Explain.*"

Sirenna set the glass down and leaned forward, resting her elbows on the table. "Most who enter the Palace surrender to their comfort. They let their minds slip, chasing pleasure or nostalgia, until they forget what they came for. It's easy to stay." Her dark eyes darted to Dunn's, daring him to disagree.

But she continued before he could.

"She didn't get lost in it. She didn't cling to illusions or beg for comfort. She didn't flinch from pain or hardship. That's how she escaped."

Dunn's jaw tightened.

"She chose freedom," Sirenna finished, her voice soft, almost indulgent, yet edged with something razor-sharp beneath it. "And most aren't that strong."

The room absorbed her words.

Dunn let the silence stretch, his mind dissecting every implication.

That girl.

He had underestimated her from the start—at the memorial, when she had been raw with grief but still held herself together. He had underestimated her again, never believing she would make it to Resonance at all. And at the Palace, when she refused to let it consume her, he had miscalculated once more. And now, she had done what no one else had.

She had moved through his world with her light.

That would not happen again.

Dunn straightened, smoothing a hand over the front of his suit, regaining control. "Then make sure it doesn't happen again."

Sirenna arched a brow.

Dunn gripped the curved top of his chair, knuckles taut, before pulling it back with a controlled scrape against the polished floor and lowering himself into the deep black leather, which huffed under his weight.

"There will be many more Watchmen entering Resonance tonight. My forces will need a direct path." His gaze locked onto Sirenna's. "Prepare the Palace. Strip it down. No comfort. I want them pushed straight through to me."

A flicker of amusement crossed Sirenna's face. "Straight to the castle?"

Dunn's lips curled. "Straight to the throne."

Sirenna nodded, the intrigue in her expression lingering. She never argued in front of an audience, but Dunn could see the gears turning in her head. She was calculating.

His soldiers would arrive soon, fresh from the real world, pulled in through his professional network, primed and eager. The moment they entered Resonance, they would be redirected.

None would get lost in the haze of dreams and indulgence. They would come straight to him.

And Sirenna would be watching.

Dunn had paid his Soul Toll long ago. He had secured his power in Resonance by betraying Ember's parents, turning against the very people who had once trusted him. Not that it weighed on him anymore. He had severed whatever remained of that part of himself. It was done. It was necessary.

But Sirenna?

She had built her influence differently. Where he had cut ties, she let them fray, unravel, tangle—keeping people bound to her, drawn in by desire, indulgence, temptation. She didn't need to betray anyone outright. She made them betray themselves.

Dunn's soldiers weren't hers, and that meant she had no hold over them. No control over what they saw, what they wanted.

Her fingers traced the rim of her glass, slow and deliberate, her gaze unreadable. Always watching. Always calculating.

Maybe she hadn't chosen a side because she didn't need to. Maybe she was still waiting to see who would win. And if that was the case, then she still had a card she hadn't played.

Or maybe she just didn't care. There would be others. This was one of many for her.

Dunn exhaled, the chandelier light cutting hard lines across his face. He had done what needed to be done—he had paid the price, and he ruled because of it.

But Sirenna hadn't paid a Soul Toll. She'd built a throne on the toll of others.

And that made her dangerous.

223

Dunn lifted his glass from the table, swirling the amber liquid inside. "Now tell me," he said, his voice quieter but no less commanding. "Where are they now?"

Next to him, Mira adjusted the tablet in front of her. The youngest of the group but sharper than most, she handled logistics with cold efficiency. She had been watching Ember's group, tracking their movements.

"They're making their way up the mountain," she said. "They moved quickly after the failed assault on the Prism."

Dunn smirked at the reminder of their failure. He had watched from his observation deck as they reached the golden cage, full of fire and conviction—only to find their weapons useless, their power meaningless against what he had built. Their light was not enough.

He would teach them what that meant.

Mira continued, "They pulled back to regroup." She tapped the screen, her tone shifting. "But here's the real problem—what if they realize they can bring the Wanderers back?"

Dunn scoffed. "The Wanderers? The husks? The remnants of those too weak to keep themselves intact?" He waved a dismissive hand. "They are nothing."

"They weren't nothing before," Mira said. "What if they remember that?"

Dunn stilled.

Slowly, he turned his gaze to her. Mira was careful—measured in her tone, her words—but she had just suggested something impossible.

"How?" Dunn stretched the word.

Mira hesitated. "What if they became… aware again." The words slid into Dunn like a slow, creeping chill, sinking deep before he could shake them off.

Awareness was the one thing he could not allow.

He had scrambled their minds, stripped them of purpose, and buried them under a relentless flood of noise and distraction—just enough to keep them drifting, never questioning, never finding their way back. They were not meant to return.

Dunn's gaze swept across the table, taking in the silent tension among his closest advisors. Hector, his warhound, was already issuing orders under his breath. Sirenna, his seductress of distraction, still held her glass delicately between her fingers, unreadable. Mira, his strategist, had planted the seed of unease, but her expression remained impassive, watching how the thought took root in Dunn's mind.

And then there were the other two.

Roland had remained silent, as he often did. Roland wasn't a man who fought battles. He was a man who funded them.

Born into wealth, he had never had to claw for survival, never had to fight for a seat at the table—he had been born at it, silver spoon already in hand. Money, power, influence—he wielded them with effortless ease, not through brute force like Hector or psychological manipulation like Sirenna, but through something more insidious: ownership.

Roland was the one who made sure Dunn's empire had resources. The infrastructure, the supply chains, the networks that made Resonance function—all of it ran through Roland's hands. He brokered deals, managed the flow of capital, and ensured that the people who needed to be paid were kept loyal. The drones Hector relied on? Roland had funded them. The Watchmen Dunn needed to deploy? Roland had made sure they were trained, equipped, and paid.

And that's why he was here.

Tonight, Roland had signed off on the single most expensive maneuver Resonance had ever seen.

Yet, as the discussion unfolded, his focus wasn't on Dunn.

Dunn caught it—the way Roland's gaze moved toward Sirenna, subtle but deliberate, lingering just long enough to be noted.

Dunn turned to him, testing. "Do you have something to add, Roland?"

Roland exhaled through his nose in something close to amusement. He set his untouched glass of wine down, adjusting the cuff of his pristine sleeve.

"I only find it… curious," he said smoothly, his voice cool and effortless. "That the Wanderers—things you so expertly hollowed out—are now something worth worrying about."

Hector's chair scraped against the floor as he leaned forward, arms braced on the table. "It's because of the drones," he said, his voice clipped, laced with irritation. "The distraction should have held them longer."

Roland hummed in mock consideration. "Yes, the drones." His fingers tapped lightly on the table. "And yet, we're moving past distraction now, aren't we?"

No one spoke.

He let his gaze drift, slow and intentional, between Dunn and Hector before finally tipping his head toward Mira. "I assume everything is in place? The helicopters. The Watchmen deployment. The parachutes." He let the word hang, amused. "Quite the... dramatic investment."

Dunn's fingers flexed against the leather armrest.

Roland leaned back, his expression unreadable. "You should be grateful that I find this venture greatly entertaining. Otherwise, I might question why we're here at all."

Hector clenched his jaw. "You don't win battles by buying them, Roland."

Roland chuckled. "No, Hector. You win them by ensuring they never need to be fought in the first place." His voice remained easy, but his words were precise. "If we had locked this down before it ever became a problem—if we had used the Watchmen from the start, instead of relying on toys and theatrics—this conversation wouldn't be necessary."

Dunn watched, listened. He understood what Roland was really saying.

Roland had financed this war. He had funded the Watchmen.

But money flowed where power did.

And if this failed? If Dunn couldn't hold what was his?

Then Roland would fund whoever could.

Dunn turned his cold gaze toward Esme. She had once been a scholar, a philosopher, a woman who had sought to understand Resonance, rather than conquer it. That had been before Dunn found her.

Her silver-blonde hair was streaked with veins of gold, as if the Prism itself had touched her. Her pale hands, resting on the arms of her chair, bore scars that shimmered when the light hit them. She had once been Dunn's greatest critic. Now, she was his most devout.

The silence stretched, thick and waiting. And then, from the far end of the table, Esme exhaled audibly.

Low. Knowing.

"You're all arguing over control," she said, unhurried. "And yet, none of you seem to realize—you don't have it."

Dunn turned to her, patience thinning. "Then tell me, Esme," he said, voice measured, "who does?"

She smiled, tilting her head. "That's what you should be asking yourself."

Roland let out a low chuckle, swirling his wine. "Ah, here we go," he said, his tone dripping with detached amusement. "Esme, weaving riddles again."

"I only weave what's already unraveling."

She leaned forward, her fingertips resting against the table, movements slow, deliberate. "You think the problem is strategy," she said. "That the failure of distraction means you need force." She gestured toward Hector without looking at him. "Or that you simply chose the wrong kind of force." Now, to Roland. "But you're all missing the bigger picture. Ember's not just resisting—she's affecting Resonance itself. Changing it."

Mira stiffened.

Dunn frowned. "Changing it how?"

Esme studied him, considering. Then, sliding her fingers against the polished wood, she said, "The light is moving."

She paused.

"And if the light moves—what do you think happens to the dark?"

The room stilled.

Dunn didn't like riddles. He especially didn't like them from Esme, because hers were never just riddles.

They were warnings.

And they were always right.

She leaned back slightly, her fingers trailing absently against the table. "I feel it." Her gaze moved to Dunn now, sharp, direct. "The shadows we cast—the ones that keep the Wanderers distracted, the ones that keep this world in check—they're thinning. The black shroud you had me weave over the Prism?" Her lips pressed together, "It's weakening."

Dunn's jaw tightened. "You told me it would hold."

"I told you it would hold as long as the balance remained the same," she corrected, her voice still calm. "But it's shifting. She's shifting it."

Roland exhaled, setting his glass down with a clink. "So let me get this straight," he mused. "All of Dunn's lovely distractions, all of his carefully laid veils, are starting to come undone?" He smirked. "Sounds expensive."

Dunn ignored him. His focus was on Esme.

She had built his control over the shadows—the tendrils of black smoke that whispered doubt into the minds of the weak, the veil that kept the Prism locked away, unreachable. She was the one who helped him control the balance of light and dark in this world, ensuring that the light never burned too bright, never became something more than he could contain.

And now, she was telling him it was slipping.

Dunn exhaled slowly, measured. "How do we fix it, Esme?"

Esme laughed softly, shaking her head. "Oh, Dunn." She tilted her head, like she almost pitied him. "You don't fix something like this. You prepare for what's coming."

Dunn's fingers drummed once against the armrest of his chair. "And what exactly is coming, Esme?"

She held his gaze, unblinking. "A shift."

"And there it is." Roland reached for his wine again, leaning back in his chair. "You know, Esme, for someone who understands so much, you really do love making it all sound like a fairy tale."

Hector scoffed, pushing back from the table. "Enough riddles. We need to move."

Sirenna stretched her arms over her head, unbothered. "She's not wrong, though," she mused. "Something is shifting." She looked to Dunn, her gaze playful but pointed. "And you can feel it, can't you?"

Dunn didn't answer.

"Enough talk," he said, tone final. "We need to move."

With that, the meeting fractured. Chairs scraped against the polished floor. Hector was the first to stand, already making his way toward the exit. Mira followed, murmuring something to him about the next steps. Sirenna lingered, exchanging one last glance with Roland before sauntering off.

Esme, true to form, said nothing else. She simply stood, her dark robes rustling against the floor as she made her way toward the door.

Only Roland remained seated, finishing his wine at a leisurely pace. He didn't look rushed. Because men like Roland were never rushed.

Dunn caught Roland's eyes as he stood.

Roland smirked, setting his glass down with an easy flick of his wrist. "Well," he mused, smoothing out his cuffs, "I do love a good gamble."

And with that, he left.

Dunn exhaled, rolling his shoulders back. The room, once full of voices and tension, fell into silence.

Then, Susan appeared in the doorway. She hesitated for a second, taking in the table, the emptied wine glasses.

"What's going on?" she asked, glancing at Dunn.

Dunn barely spared her a look as he stood. "Nothing that concerns you," he said simply.

Her brow furrowed, but before she could press, he waved a dismissive hand. "Go home, Susan."

And without another word, she turned and left.

CHAPTER 40

FOUND

The morning mist clung to the trees as Ember, Jade, Derek, and Frank packed up and started down the mountain trail. The air smelled of wet earth and pine, the ground still soft from last night's rain.

"Ugh, I hate having to go back to go forward."

Jade popped a berry into her mouth, stepping over a thick root. "Better than standing still."

"I know, I know, it's the only way," Ember went on, rolling her head side to side to crack her neck. "But it feels backward. Like we're undoing progress just to make some."

Derek smirked. "You do like to ramble."

Ember shot him a look. "It's not rambling, it's processing. I talk through things—it helps me sort them out." She lifted her chin. "It's my process."

Derek raised a brow. "Sounds a lot like—"

"Shut up!" Ember smiled.

The dirt-packed path curved downward, weaving between jagged rock formations and dense trees. Every so often, Ember caught movement in the underbrush, a bird shifting in the shadows, a rabbit darting into the ferns, but something about the forest felt... still.

Frank trotted ahead, ears flicking at the occasional rustle, his damp scarf wrapped around his chest.

"Feels weird, doesn't it?" Jade muttered.

"Yeah," Ember murmured, running her fingers over the gold chain burned into her wrist. The skin underneath was still tender.

The further they walked, the heavier the air felt. Not in weight but in presence. Like they were moving toward something, even as the path pulled them away from the mountain's peak.

Then Frank stopped. His body tensed, ears pinned forward. He didn't growl. Didn't bark. Just stood completely still, nose twitching at something ahead.

Derek's voice dropped. "What is it, boy?"

Frank took a slow step forward, then another. Ember strained to hear what had set him off, but the forest was silent. No birds, no wind. Just the sound of her own breath.

Then she saw it—the break in the trees ahead. The place where the forest thinned, and the world beyond would come into view.

She exhaled and took a step forward.

The Wanderers weren't waiting for them.

But they were about to be found.

CHAPTER 41

COMING TOGETHER

The path stretched ahead, winding through a landscape drained of color. Ember led the way, her boots scuffing against dry, cracked ground. Derek followed beside her, and Jade trailed just behind. Frank trotted ahead, nose twitching as he sniffed at the air, looking back occasionally to check on the group.

Then, the voices drifted toward them—distant murmurs carried by the wind. Ember slowed, and Derek tensed at her side.

"We're here," she said quietly.

They stepped over the last ridge and looked down at the Wanderers.

A sea of people moved below, their forms shifting without pattern or urgency, lost in the haze of their own minds. Their faces were blank, eyes fixed somewhere beyond the present. Some paced in endless circles. Others stood completely still, their expressions vacant. And above each head, wisps of thought unraveled like curling tendrils of smoke, rising toward the sky. The tendrils stretched higher and higher until they disappeared into the void.

Frank let out a low whine, uneasy.

"They don't see us," Jade said. "They don't see anything."

"They're... gone," Derek added.

Ember inhaled. *No. Not gone. Not yet.*

She stepped forward. "I need to touch their hearts."

Derek shot her a skeptical look. "And how exactly do you plan to do that?"

Ember didn't answer right away. Instead, she closed her eyes, centering herself. And then walked down to the center of the clearing, as the others followed.

The Wanderers milled around the group in that same distant fog, thoughts drifting from their heads in spectral wisps, stretching endlessly toward the sky.

Jade stood a few feet behind Ember, her arms wrapped around herself, her brows pinched with doubt. "Every time I think I've seen the limits of this place...," she muttered, watching the lifeless figures shuffle past.

Frank's ears flicked as he let out a low whine. He prowled forward, sniffing at the feet of a man who didn't even flinch at his presence.

Ember planted her feet. She could feel the weight of the moment. Then, she inhaled deeply and let her voice rise into the empty air.

It started soft—a thread of sound barely audible over the wind. A single note, held long and steady, vibrating in her chest like something ancient, something known.

Then the melody took shape.

Come back down, feel the earth,
Let the quiet pull you close.
The storm in your mind will keep raging,
But your heart knows where to go.

The first few notes drifted through the air, curling around the Wanderers. Nothing happened. Their empty eyes still stared through her, their bodies still moving without thought or intention.

Jade shifted uncomfortably. Derek frowned. Frank sat beside Ember, his tail thumping against the dust.

Ember continued, her voice weaving into something fuller, stronger, a song meant to guide them out of the dark.

Thoughts will pull, thoughts will spin,
Tangled threads of endless sound.
But listen low—listen deeper—
Can you hear your heartbeat now?

A man in the crowd stopped. His face twitched. His head tilted, as though a forgotten memory had brushed against him.

Jade sucked in a breath.

Then a woman gasped. Her hand fluttered to her chest, her lips parting in an unspoken question.

Derek tensed. "It's working."

One by one, the Wanderers stilled, the tendrils of thought trailing from their heads beginning to dissolve into the air. The more Ember sang, the more they turned toward her, eyes widening, their breath deepening. Their hands clenched, their fingers flexed, their feet stopped their endless pacing.

Something was shifting.

Something was waking.

By the time she reached the final words, the silence was so absolute it swallowed even the sound of the wind.

Breathe back in, fall back home,
Let the weight of knowing go.
The mind may wander, but the heart remains—
Let your light take root and grow.

The last note faded. For a breathless moment, the Wanderers stood frozen. Silence hung between them. Then, from somewhere deep in the crowd, a single drumbeat sounded.

Boom.

Ember turned toward the sound.

The group parted, revealing a man seated at the center. He sat on the ground, legs crossed, a large drum resting between his knees. His hands hovered over the taut surface of the hide. A silver ring gleamed on one of his fingers, a contrast to the dust smudged along his arms. His skin was deep brown, lined with years of wisdom and hardship, his eyes gleamed with something Ember recognized immediately—understanding. And as he raised his hand again, he brought it down with purpose.

Boom.

Another beat, steady and low, reverberated through the air.

Suddenly, Ember knew exactly what to do.

The rhythm grew and seeped into her bones, slow at first, then insistent. Her body responded instinctively, moving in time with the pulse. The vibrations settled in her core, spreading down to her legs, urging her to move. It was primal, raw—a connection to something greater than herself.

She began to dance.

Boom.

Her body responded.

At first, it was subtle—a roll of her shoulders, a shift of her hips. Then, as the drumbeat intensified, the movement took over. Her arms swept through the air, her spine undulating, her feet gliding across the dust. The pulse of the rhythm commanded every part of her, aligning her with the deep, unshaken truth of her own existence.

Light burst from her chest, bright and raw, radiating outward.

The others stared in wonder, at the clarity of their minds, and the light of Ember's heart, and couldn't resist, they joined in her movement.

First, it was just a handful of them. The newly awakened. Their feet hesitated at first, but the rhythm was undeniable. They swayed, then stepped, then spun, hands reaching toward the sky.

Then the drumming quickened, and more came.

Figures emerged from the tree line beyond the clearing, drawn by the sound, their eyes clearing as they moved. Dozens, then hundreds. The space swelled with bodies, their once-lost movements turning into something powerful, intentional, real. The barren wasteland that had been empty moments before now pulsed with movement, with breath, with life.

Derek was grinning. "You're seeing this, right?"

Jade exhaled in disbelief and turned to Derek. "This is… this is unreal!"

Frank barked and leapt into the frenzy, weaving between the dancers, his tail wagging wildly.

The drumbeat was intoxicating. Ember spun, her arms opening wide, embracing the sheer aliveness of it. She let the light from her heart expand, filling the clearing, flooding over the Wanderers, wrapping them in something they had forgotten existed.

The dance reached its peak.

And then, as suddenly as it had begun, it stopped.

Ember froze in place, her breath heaving.

The clearing was full. Completely full.

Hundreds—no, thousands—of people stood before her. Not just the ones she had found. Not just the ones from the woods. Others had come. Some had been lost for days, others for years.

And every single one of them stared at her with clear, awakened eyes.

She swallowed hard.

A man stepped forward, his hands trembling at his sides. His voice cracked. "Who… who are you?"

Murmurs rippled through the crowd. Others echoed the same question.

"What just happened?"

"What did you do?"

Ember looked out at them. The weight of their expectation pressed on her, but she wasn't afraid. Not anymore.

"You were trapped," she said simply. "Wandering, lost in distraction. But we called you home."

A woman in the crowd choked out a sob.

Another man brought his hands to his forehead, his fingers shaking. "My mind… it's quiet."

A young girl, barely more than a teenager, whispered, "I thought I was dead."

Murmurs rose again.

Jade straightened. "You tried to fight before. And you lost. But this time... we don't fight alone."

Silence settled. A ripple of understanding passed through the crowd. Then the drummer spoke, his voice low, firm. "Then tell us. What comes next?"

Ember looked at Jade. At Derek. At Frank, who stood panting at her feet. Then she turned back to the crowd. "We go back up that mountain," she said. "Together."

And the Wanderers—once lost, now found—answered with a roar.

CHAPTER 42

GROUNDING DOWN

The air had shifted.

The heavy silence that once smothered the Wanderers had lifted, replaced by excited murmurs and the steady rhythm of conscious breath. The crisp scent of cooling earth mingled with something else—anticipation. The sky overhead was a steel-gray expanse, but for the first time in a long time, the Wanderers weren't staring into it like lost souls waiting for something to pull them upward. They were here. Grounded. Listening.

Ember stood before them, her boots planted firmly. The crowd encircled her, faces illuminated by the late-afternoon light. She saw in their eyes—some of them still afraid, some blinking like they'd just woken up, and others filled with something fierce, something alive.

"We tried before," Ember began, her voice carrying across the clearing. "Derek and I climbed the mountain. We faced Dunn. We thought we could restore the Prism on our own." She let the weight of that admission settle over them. "And we failed."

A ripple moved through the crowd, quiet but unmistakable.

She raised her hands. "I know what you're thinking. That you've already tried, too. That you were the ones who tried. That you made the climb, and you were lost for it." Her eyes scanned the crowd, settling on the man she recognized.

He was thin, his beard uneven. His clothes hung loose, his movements hesitant, but there was clarity in his gaze now. And when she spoke again, she directed it to him.

"You tried to warn us."

He stiffened, shifting his weight. His hands curled at his sides. "I tried," he rasped, his voice dry from years of silence. Then he lifted his arm, his index finger trembling as he pointed up. "Up," he said, a note of fear coiling through the word. His gaze lifted, his body tensing as if waiting for something unseen to strike from above.

Ember followed his line of sight. The sky.

The moment snapped into place.

The first time they'd encountered him, she had thought he was urging them to keep going. To continue their ascent.

But he hadn't been pointing at the mountain.

He had been pointing at the drones.

"Up!" she echoed, nodding in realization. "You weren't telling us to go. You were warning us to look up. The drones."

The man exhaled through his nose, his lips pressing into a tight line. Then he nodded.

Derek let out a low whistle beside her.

Ember turned back to the crowd. "I wish I had been clever enough to understand you," she said. "Thank you."

A woman stepped forward. "If the drones are still there… if Dunn is still waiting…" Her voice wavered, and she gripped her own wrist, as if bracing herself. "How do we know it won't happen again?"

Ember met her gaze. "Because much has changed." She stepped forward, closer to them. "Neither Derek nor I became Wanderers. We may have failed at restoring the Prism, but we got one thing right—we did not lose ourselves."

The woman stared at her. Others whispered. Someone from the back of the crowd called, "But *how*?"

Ember turned toward Jade.

"This is Jade," she announced. "She's a doctor and a healer. A real one." She smiled at Jade, who gave her a wry look in return. "She prepared us before we made our attempt. And she will do the same for all of you now."

Jade stepped forward, hands on her hips. "You're damn right I will," she said, scanning the crowd like she was assessing a room of patients. "You've had your minds pulled from you once before. We're going to make sure it doesn't happen again."

Ember nodded. "We don't have much time. We'll leave at dusk."

There was a pause. Then, one by one, heads began to nod. The group was on board.

A wave of motion rippled through them. Some turned to each other, grasping hands, pulling one another into tight, shaking embraces—reunions after years spent in the fog. Others moved toward Jade, listening intently as she began directing them.

And then there was Frank. A small group of Wanderers knelt beside him, scratching his ears, rubbing his shoulders, murmuring in hushed voices as if he carried some kind of quiet wisdom. Frank, ever the diplomat, basked in the attention, tail thudding happily against the dust.

Ember chuckled as she watched.

Derek elbowed her lightly. "Guess he's the real hero of the rebellion."

They walked together, stepping back from the main throng, their boots crunching against the dirt. The clearing was more alive now than ever. Ember let herself take it in.

Derek exhaled, then cast her a sidelong glance. "Do you really think we can do it?" He lifted his hands before she could answer. "Not that I'm afraid. Just... making conversation."

Ember smiled. "It all feels right, Derek. It's all in alignment." She let out a slow breath. "Yes. We will do it."

They passed a group gathered near the edges of the clearing where Jade was already preparing her ritual.

Bundles of herbs, carefully selected and bound, were laid in neat rows along a makeshift altar of stacked stones. The scent of dried sage and wild lavender filled the air, mingling with the crisp, mineral bite of the approaching dusk.

Jade knelt beside the arrangement, drawing careful patterns into the dirt with her fingertips. Around her, a circle of Wanderers stood in quiet reverence, their hands linked. Her voice carried through the air—not loud, not insistent, but certain.

Ember watched.

Jade reached into the folds of her clothes and withdrew a small satchel, pulling free a vial of shimmering liquid. She unstoppered it, let a single drop spill onto the earth, and then whispered something in a language Ember didn't recognize.

A slow pulse, deep and thrumming, spread outward from the center of the circle. The earth beneath their feet seemed to settle, humming, as if it were breathing.

Jade looked up, her gaze meeting Ember's across the distance. She didn't say anything. She didn't need to.

This was happening.

CHAPTER 43

WARRIOR ONE

The last light of day stretched thin across the sky. Ember sat on a fallen log, her fingers tracing the gold chain wrapped around her wrist. It was warm—not from the lingering heat of the sun, but from something else. Something unseen.

It pulsed, steady and deliberate, a tether she had yet to understand.

She twisted it, testing for weakness, for meaning hidden in its gleaming surface. Was it a restraint? A mark? Or something worse—a leash Dunn could tighten the moment she got too close?

Frank sat at her feet. He let out a low huff, nudging her knee with his nose as if to say, *Enough with that.*

Ember exhaled. "Yeah, yeah, I hear you."

Before she could think too much more, Derek's voice cut in. "Alright, Ember. We're ready."

She looked up. The Wanderers had gathered, forming a massive semicircle in the clearing. Some still looked uneasy, but beneath it, she saw conviction.

Ember took her place in the front of them, and they hushed. She stood firm and scanned the crowd, searching each face, making sure they knew she saw them. Then she spoke.

"We tried before. And we lost."

The words hung, heavy in the air. A fire crackled in the silence.

"We caught Dunn by surprise, and even that wasn't enough. He had already built his defenses, already turned his fortress into a trap. And when we got there—when we thought we had a chance to free the Prism—we weren't ready. We were strong. But not strong enough. We weren't together the way we needed to be."

She took a step forward. "Dunn has been amassing an army. We saw them. He's not just relying on drones anymore. He's bringing in troops through Sirenna's palace, and who knows how many more are coming? This time, he will be prepared."

Fear passed over the crowd, but Ember didn't let it settle.

"And so are we."

Silence. Stillness. Then, the shift.

"We are not the same people we were before," Ember continued, her voice gaining strength. "We are not just fighting with light—we are the light. We are the ones who have seen what happens when fear takes hold, when the world turns to distraction, to control, to emptiness. But we have also seen what happens when we break free. When we stand together. When we rise."

She turned, meeting the gaze of the drummer from before. He sat cross-legged, his hands resting on the taut surface of his instrument, waiting.

"When we make this climb, we do it together. We do it knowing what's at stake. And we do it knowing that we cannot be stopped."

Ember spread her arms wide. "Now, let's come together. Feel it. Stand in it."

She stepped backward, motioning for them to move with her. Slowly, they did.

"Find your feet. Feel the ground beneath you. The earth that holds you, the body that moves with you. This is where we begin."

Ember lifted her arms, shifting into Warrior Pose, and the others followed.

A sea of bodies stretched into the clearing, every stance strong, every breath deep.

Ember walked among them, guiding, adjusting postures, deepening her connection with them. "Let your breath move with you. Let your heart push outward. Be here. In this moment."

From Warrior, they shifted into Goddess Pose, their arms raised, their chests open, their legs powerful.

Their bodies began to shimmer—not with sweat, but with something deeper.

Light.

One by one, the golden threads of their inner radiance began to unfurl.

Jade stepped forward, her own energy crackling. "Feel it," she called out. "Not just in yourself. In the person beside you. In the people behind you. We are not alone in this."

Ember watched as the Wanderers, once broken, once lost, turned their heads and saw one another. Not just as strangers. Not just as survivors.

As something greater.

A low hum filled the air—not from words, but from the resonance of breath, of movement, of presence.

It built.

It grew.

And then, all at once, the lights of their hearts ignited.

Golden light flickered beneath their skin, weaving through their limbs, pulsing with each inhale, each exhale. Their energy linked, an unseen current humming between them, as bright as the fire, as steady as the mountain beneath their feet.

Sonder.

Every life, every path, connected. Every heartbeat an echo of another.

Frank let out a sharp bark, his tail wagging furiously. The energy made the fur along his back stand on end, and he spun in a circle before bounding toward Derek, panting with excitement.

Derek chuckled, rubbing Frank's head, and laughter rippled through the Wanderers—tentative at first, then rising into something unmistakeable. Joy.

Ember inhaled deeply, then exhaled.

"We're ready."

The moment lingered, golden and whole, and the first beat of the drum struck.

Boom.

The Wanderers turned. The drummer's hands moved, slow at first, then faster. The rhythm grew, low and rolling, stirring something in the earth beneath them.

Then, as if drawn by the pulse, the crowd shifted.

Bodies moved, gathering their things. Hands brushed against arms, steadying each other. Ember turned to Derek and he met her gaze, lifting an eyebrow.

"No turning back now," he said.

She smiled. "Wouldn't dream of it."

And then, all together, they stepped onto the path. The trail wound ahead, the mountain looming, waiting. In almost an instant, as one, they became a river of gold snaking up the trail.

They were coming—out loud, out in the open, with light bursting from their hearts and the thunder of the drum shaking the ground beneath their feet. They weren't hiding. They weren't sneaking.

They were rising, and the whole world would know it.

CHAPTER 44

RIVER OF LIGHT

The mountain had never burned so brightly.

The Wanderers stretched across the jagged ridge, a river of golden light against the darkening sky. Their bodies pulsed with energy, their breath synchronized with the steady thunder of the drums. The rhythm pushed them forward, a force as old as the mountain itself, as unstoppable as the tide.

The climb had been long, their bodies aching, but Ember didn't slow. Neither did the others.

Above them, the peak loomed, silhouetted against a sky streaked with the final shreds of sunset. Wisps of cloud curled around its jagged cliffs, glowing red, orange, and gold in the dying light. Higher still, Dunn's fortress stood like an omen against the encroaching night.

Ember led the charge, her boots striking firm against the loose stone. Her breath came steady, strong. She could hear Derek just behind her, Jade a few strides to her left, the Wanderers spreading wide behind them, stretching the length of the path. Frank bounded ahead, weaving between their legs, his nose low to the ground.

A low wind curled through the mountain pass, when the first drone appeared.

Several Wanderers stiffened, shoulders tensing as their eyes darted toward one another. The drones had taken them before—had stolen their minds, had turned them into nothing but hollow shells.

Ember felt the presence of fear behind her.

A surge of black tendrils lashed through the air, twisting like shadows. One struck a Wanderer—a gaunt man with sunken eyes, his skin stretched tight over sharp bones. The tendrils wrapped around his head, curling tight, sinking into him like ink bleeding into water—and then, they vanished.

Silence fell over the mountain.

The man stood taller, his breath steady. Then, slowly, he lifted his arms into the air, victorious.

Above, the drones jerked, their sensors flickering erratically. They stuttered midair, recalibrated, then shuddered again— power failing, systems collapsing.

One by one, they dropped.

A roar of triumph tore through the Wanderers.

Voices whooped, wild and unrestrained. Hands clapped against backs, fists punched the air. Someone let out a scream— not of fear, but of victory.

The drones—the things that had hunted and broken them— were nothing now.

Frank barked, leaping forward, tail wagging furiously as he spun in wild circles. Ember couldn't help the grin that spread across her face.

"They don't work on us anymore," Derek said in awe.

"No," Ember agreed, her eyes burning. "They don't."

The fire inside them flared, their light burning even brighter. For the first time, they could taste victory.

And then, the mountain screamed.

A piercing, mechanical whine cut through the cheers. The ground shuddered beneath them, and in an instant, the celebration froze.

From the cliffs above, the Watchmen emerged—silent, disciplined, relentless.

And then they struck. With a flick of their wrists, golden chains cracked through the air like whips and found wrists, ankles, throats, locking tight the moment they found flesh.

The first line of Wanderers collapsed, and a strangled cry ripped through the air.

Then another.

The celebration shattered.

More chains shot from the fortress above, their golden glow blinding as they spiraled downward. They wrapped around legs, pinned arms, dragged bodies to the ground.

Ember spun, breath caught in her chest as the battlefield turned.

Where there had just been strength, now there was chaos.

Dunn's army had arrived.

The Watchmen moved in formation, emerging from the cliffs, their armor gleaming with golden circuitry. Their movements were cold, calculated—fighters engineered for one thing: control.

The golden chains rippled in the air, tightening, constricting.

Some of the Wanderers fought back, their light flaring as they tried to rip free. Others reached for their fallen, trying to pry the bindings loose. But for each one that broke free, another fell.

More and more were being caught.

•◆•

And high above them, Dunn watched.

He stood on his observation deck, hands folded behind his back, his sharp suit untouched by the violence unfolding below.

His lips curled as he watched the golden wires coil around their prey. He turned, and his gaze settled on the Prism. It sat within its protective cage, coated in black, its glow strong but contained. Guards now stood at every entrance, with their weapons drawn.

Dunn let out a slow breath.

"No way in," he mused.

His victory was secure.

And then—he felt it.

He turned, eyes scanning the battlefield, and there she was. Ember.

She wasn't watching the fight. She wasn't watching the fallen. She was watching him, and she had noticed something.

•◆•

Ember turned, gripping Derek's arm. "You have to lead them."

Derek blinked. "What?"

"Lead them to the Prism. There's something we missed, something I need to do."

His jaw clenched. "Ember—"

But she was already gone. Slipping between the struggle, weaving through the chaos before he could stop her.

Derek cursed under his breath, and then turned, scanning the battlefield, the golden-lit mountain, the bodies rising and falling. He had no choice. He let out a breath, set his shoulders, and then he raised his voice.

"KEEP MOVING!"

He reached for Jade, pulling her up from where she had been shielding a fallen Wanderer. "Help the others get to the Prism!"

Jade's breath was ragged, but she nodded, gripping his wrist before she turned, rallying those who could still fight.

The battle raged around them, but they pressed forward.

Step by step.

Breath by breath.

More golden chains whipped out, more bodies fell.

The climb was getting harder.

CHAPTER 45

THE CASTLE

The corridors of the castle stretched long and cold before Ember, the dim light casting warped shadows along the walls. The air smelled of polished stone, dust, and something metallic, like dried blood. She moved quickly, her footsteps hushed against the marble.

Then she saw her.

Susan.

She stood at the end of the hall, leaning against an ornate column, her arms folded over her chest with a brace on her wrist. The golden light from the battle outside moved across her face, her expression was unreadable.

Ember slowed. Her heart pounded. "Susan?"

Susan exhaled and stepped forward. "Seriously?"

Ember shook her head. "What the hell are you doing here?"

Susan sighed, running a hand through her hair. "I'm sorry, Ember."

A chill passed through her. "You're sorry?"

Susan's lips pressed into a thin line. "We all have to make our choices."

Ember swallowed the sting that curled inside her. She had no time for this. No time for explanations, for betrayals, for the ache of losing yet another person to Dunn's grasp.

She stepped past Susan without another word, and Susan didn't stop her.

The observation deck loomed ahead, and Ember could hear the soft clink of glass before she even saw him.

Dunn.

He stood at the edge, a glass of something dark in his hand, swirling the liquid absently before taking a slow sip. His golden bracelet caught the light as he lifted his wrist, the soft metallic chime punctuating the silence.

This man killed my parents.

Her stomach twisted, hot with hatred, burning with a rage so pure she could taste it. She curled her fingers into fists. Every muscle in her body screamed for her to strike, to shatter him like he had shattered her life.

She then realized she was holding her breath and remembered to breathe.

I inhale. I exhale.

The air filled her lungs. The moment steadied beneath her.

She gathered her courage, lifted her chin, and stepped forward.

The sound of her boots against the marble made Dunn turn. His eyes widened for the briefest moment before his fingers slipped, and his glass tumbled from his hand, shattering at his feet.

"What are you doing here?" Then Dunn laughed, like he was trying to mask his surprise. "Right to the lion's den? Ha! You just couldn't stay in line, could you?"

Ember took a step forward, unfazed. "Looks like I made it fast enough after all, Dunn."

His eyes narrowed. "Now how is that?" He gestured to the battlefield below, where the golden chains still coiled around the Wanderers, binding them. "I see your nice little show down there, Ember." He turned back to her, shaking his head like a disappointed father. "But I'm the one standing here with the upper hand. You've done nothing but put a lot of people in danger. Nice work."

He turned, dismissing her, his eyes back on the battle.

Ember's rage flared.

"You killed my parents, Dunn." Her voice was steel.

Dunn stilled.

"And you thought you could tame me."

Slowly, he turned to face her. The amusement was gone from his face.

Ember took another step forward. He stepped back, away from the balcony, closer to the castle.

"But I am the spark you could not snuff out." She leaned in. He stepped back again. "I remembered who I am, Dunn. And now, I stand in my own light, beyond your reach."

His lips curled into something dangerous. "You think you're beyond me?" he spat. "You think you've won?"

He stepped forward this time, closing the space between them in a single breath. His presence was heavy, suffocating, but Ember didn't flinch.

"You can't stop this," he sneered. "You're just a girl playing with fire."

Ember exhaled.

She stood her ground, looked him in the eyes and declared: "You have no control over me."

And with those words, the gold chain around her wrist loosened and fell, clattering on the stone floor.

Dunn's expression cracked, rage twisting his features. "No—"

He lunged towards her.

Before he could reach her, a blur of fur and fangs slammed into him

Frank.

The dog hit hard, his jaws clamping onto Dunn's wrist. Teeth met metal and he snapped the gold bracelet clean off.

Dunn let out a furious roar, his body twisting as Frank landed hard, rolling straight toward the edge of the balcony.

Ember's heart stopped.

"FRANK!"

His paws scrambled against the slick stone, claws scraping, searching for grip—but he slipped over the edge.

Ember and Dunn lunged in the same direction, but while Ember was after Frank, Dunn's eyes were locked on the cage.

The golden gate burst open as the cage tipped back, falling away, leaving the Prism exposed.

Dunn's voice shattered the air. "NO!"

The Prism awoke.

A blinding light exploded from the broken cage, a single, searing beam piercing the sky.

Every Wanderer, still bound in golden chains, began to glow—not with restraint, but with something greater, something unleashed. The light from their hearts ignited, surging outward in a brilliant cascade, merging into a radiant beam that shot toward the Prism. The black shroud that had smothered it began to dissolve and melted away.

The Prism emerged, untouched, unbroken.

And magnificent.

It contained and refracted every color of the universe. Its light spread in waves, illuminating everything, pushing back the darkness, dissolving the golden bindings that had held the Wanderers captive.

Ember gasped at the brilliance of the vision.

Dunn staggered back. His face twisted in fury, his hands clawing at the air as if he could will the cage to close again. His breath came in ragged gasps.

"You stupid girl," he snarled, his eyes locking onto Ember.

He lunged at her and just as he was about to make contact—he vanished.

Ember blinked, her pulse hammering in her ears. She looked out to the mountain, but the battlefield below wasn't a battlefield anymore.

Dunn's entire army was gone. The Wanderers who had been bound now simply brushed the golden threads away.

A breath shuddered through her, the weight of everything crashing into her at once.

Then, she remembered.

Frank.

Her stomach twisted. She ran to the edge of the balcony, scanning the jagged rocks below.

But he wasn't there.

Her heart dropped.

No. No, no, no.

Then—movement.

A small figure trotting steadily across the stone, tail wagging, ears bouncing with each step. And around his neck—

A colorful scarf.

"Frank!" She shouted as a half-laugh, half-sob, broke from her throat.

She turned and sprinted through the castle toward him, toward the others, toward everything waiting beyond this moment.

CHAPTER 46

THE PRISM

The air around the Prism shimmered, pulsing with color that rippled outward like waves in a cosmic ocean. Ember stepped forward, breathless, feeling the warmth radiating from its core. The crystalline structure hovered just above the stone platform, its edges refracting every shade of the spectrum. Inside, swirling light moved like a living thing, shifting between forms, ancient and powerful.

She turned to Derek and Jade. They stood beside her, their faces caught in the glow.

"We actually did it," Derek said, shaking his head in disbelief. His arms hung at his sides, knuckles still bruised from the fight, but there was something in his stance—something lighter. "It's real. It's here."

Jade exhaled. "I've studied energy, light, the body's connection to it all—but this…" She gestured at the Prism, her fingers trembling. "This is beyond everything I thought I knew."

Ember let her gaze travel up the Prism's perfect edges. It was beautiful in a way that made her chest ache.

A cool breeze swept through the mountaintop, carrying the scent of rain even though the sky was clear. Below them, the mountain stretched into shadow, the golden battlefield now calm. The Wanderers, freed from their chains, stood at the edges of the platform, silent and in awe.

Frank trotted forward, sniffing at the Prism, then sneezed. His ears perked, and he wagged his tail, as if understanding something the rest of them hadn't yet caught.

Then,

A pulse.

A single, concentrated beam of light streamed from the Prism, a cosmic ribbon of color unfurling across the sky, stretching toward the base of the mountain in a slow, radiant cascade.

The ground beneath their feet trembled, but it wasn't fear that gripped Ember—it was knowing.

The Prism wasn't just awakening.

It was calling them home.

A hum built in the air, vibrating through their bones. Ember turned to Derek and Jade. "Do you feel that?"

Jade nodded, eyes wide. "It's pulling us."

Derek cracked a grin. "Well, if this thing wants to give us a lift, I say we take it."

Ember laughed, a wild, unrestrained sound. Then she reached out her hand. "Together?"

Derek took it without hesitation. Jade followed, gripping Ember's other hand. Around them, the Wanderers stepped forward, linking arms, joining the connection.

The light surged, wrapping around their feet, swirling up their legs. It didn't burn. It didn't sting. It was warmth, comfort, and exhilaration all at once. It was electric.

Then, the world dropped away.

The Prism's energy carried them downward in a stream of brilliance, the wind rushing past but never cold. It was effortless, weightless, as though they had become part of the light itself. The stars blurred, the night split open with color.

The mountain sped past, and Ember could see the Breathers waiting below.

Their eyes lifted toward the sky, their faces bathed in the descending light.

A cheer rose, swelling like a wave.

The Wanderers had returned.

The battle was over.

And they had won.

CHAPTER 47

RAINING LIGHT

The sky cracked open.

The Breathers, the festivalgoers who had waited, who had fought in their own quiet way, now stood beneath the deluge of pure light. As it touched them, their bodies responded—colors rippling across their skin, warmth blooming in their chests. Some fell to their knees, overwhelmed. Others reached toward the sky, their fingers catching the glow like fireflies.

From the peak of the mountain, the Prism's radiant glow fractured into countless dazzling beams. The light didn't fall like rain—it became the rain, droplets of brilliance descending from the heavens, dissolving into the skin of every person gathered below.

Gasps filled the air.

The festival grounds transformed before their eyes. The once-faint hum of music swelled into a euphoric symphony, resonating with the pulse of the Prism. The ground itself shimmered, alive with color, like geometric mats glowing beneath their bare feet.

Laughter rose. Then cheers. Then movement.

Ember stood at the center of it all, watching as light wove through the people, restoring what had been lost.

Joy emerged from the crowd, her wide eyes reflecting every shifting hue of the Prism.

"Ember," she exhaled, stepping closer, her hands pressing against her heart. "It's—you did it."

Ember shook her head, smiling. "We all did."

Joy turned in a slow circle, taking it all in. "This is real." She laughed then, tipping her head back, arms wide. "I knew it was real, but now—I feel it!"

A cluster of people near them collapsed into a joyous heap, laughing and crying as their light flared, fully restored. Others twirled, embracing the rain of illumination as though it were cleansing them from the inside out.

And then—music.

Not just from the speakers, but from the people themselves. Drums, voices, rhythms that had been buried beneath doubt now rising, claiming space.

Derek stepped up beside Ember, his gaze sweeping over the festival. "So… this is what winning looks like?"

She grinned. "This is what living looks like."

Derek exhaled, running a hand through his hair. His body was still bruised from the battle, his shirt torn at the sleeve, but he looked… light. Lighter than she'd ever seen him.

Then, his expression shifted.

His gaze landed on a woman near the edge of the glowing crowd—Brianna. She had sent Derek off on this journey, told him she'd be thinking of him. The one who had been part of his past, before all of this. Derek hadn't thought of her once, until now.

Brianna was laughing, her arms looped around the shoulders of someone else, her head tilted as she swayed to the music.

Derek hesitated, then stepped toward her.

Ember watched as Brianna turned, catching sight of him.

For a moment, there was a flicker of something unspoken.

Then—she smiled.

A small, knowing smile.

Derek smiled back, giving her a slight nod.

And that was it.

A casual wave-off of the past. A mutual acknowledgment.

Ember felt something ease in her chest as Derek turned back toward her, shaking his head. "Well," he said, "I guess I'm really free now."

She raised an eyebrow. "And how does that feel?"

Derek exhaled, looking at her.

"Like I should dance." He grinned.

Ember laughed as he grabbed her hand, pulling her toward the center where the pulse of the festival had transformed into something wilder.

The people around them swayed and spun, bodies painted in liquid light. Every movement left behind trails of color— auras shifting with the music, feet tracing ephemeral patterns into the illuminated earth.

Ember followed Derek's lead, her body falling into rhythm, her heart pounding with something new.

Something electric.

The air between them changed.

She could feel it in the way he looked at her, the way their hands lingered a second longer than necessary, the way his breath hitched when she spun too close.

The festival melted away, and it was just them.

"You know, we never really had a chance to—"

Ember leaned in.

And kissed him.

The music swelled.

The Prism pulsed.

And for the first time in a long time—

Everything was exactly as it should be.

CHAPTER 48

THE RETURN

Jade stood beneath a tall tree at the edge of the clearing, surrounded by a small circle of people. She guided them through breath-work as the air shimmered with warmth, laughter still drifting up from the festival in the valley below. Firelight danced across faces, and something lighter—freer—moved through the space.

Her hands moved with purpose, grinding herbs in a wooden bowl, then tying a small bundle with twine before pressing it into the hands of a young woman whose light still flickered.

She moved with an ease Ember hadn't seen in her before. No tension in her shoulders. No trace of the careful line she used to walk between her medical training and something older. She looked settled, like she'd stopped choosing between parts of herself. And whatever she was offering, the people around her leaned in, open to it.

Jade looked up and caught Ember's gaze across the trees. Her smile was small but sure, the kind that said everything was as it should be. She gave a slow nod—steady, grounded, whole.

Ember felt the weight of it. Gratitude. Recognition. A silent promise that what they'd built together would last.

She nodded back.

And then she crossed the threshold.

•◆•

The world was still.

Soft earth cradled Ember's body, the familiar scent of damp soil and pine wrapping around her. A gentle breeze wove through the trees, rustling the leaves above, their shadows shifting across her skin.

She exhaled, forehead pressed against the rubber beneath her—her mother's mat.

The air felt lighter, like the weight of something vast had finally lifted. The Prism's glow still lingered in her bones, a quiet hum beneath her skin. But here, in the hush of the forest, there was only her breath. Only Ember.

She pulled her hands in, pressing against the mat, and slowly sat back onto her heels.

Her heart still beat with the rhythm of everything that had come before. The mountain. The fall of the drones. The breaking of the golden chains. The festival—laughter, light, Derek.

She inhaled deeply, taking in the scent of pine, of earth warmed by fading sunlight. The sky above was streaked with the last hues of twilight, stars just beginning to emerge. Fireflies blinked between the trees.

She closed her eyes for a moment, listening.

The wind carried whispers of the past, echoes of those who had come before her. The ones who had walked this path, who had fought, who had lost and found themselves again.

And she knew.
She knew exactly what to do.
Ember opened her eyes.
And she rose.

CHAPTER 49

THE CURTAIN DROPS

S he stepped off the train, her feet moving on autopilot toward the glass doors she had passed through hundreds of times. The ones that led her into a space where time felt different— faster, heavier. The kind of place where the days blurred, the nights disappeared, and weeks collapsed into an unbroken loop of late hours and redlined documents.

The building was colder than usual. Or maybe Ember was just noticing it for the first time.

Because today was different.

I am going to quit my job today.

The thought pulsed through her, steady, insistent, drowning out everything else.

She walked through the marble lobby, past the security desk, into the elevator packed with silent professionals in sharp suits and worn expressions. No one spoke. They rarely did. Just phones, shifting feet, the artificial hum of air conditioning.

The elevator dinged and the doors opened.

She stepped out.

Her office felt the same, with the static hum of fluorescent lights, the distant clatter of a printer, and the smell of coffee burned hours ago.

But something had already shifted.

She didn't set down her bag. She didn't open her laptop.

Instead, she turned and started down the hall toward the Chair of her practice group. He barely looked up when she entered. His desk was spotless. "Morning, Ember. We've been wondering when you'd be back. I hope you're taking the time you need—but some communication would've helped."

She didn't sit. "I'm resigning."

His pen paused mid-signature and he lifted his gaze. Ember waited, half-expecting some kind of challenge. But it didn't come. Instead, his expression barely changed—just a slow, measuring nod before he leaned back in his chair. "You're sure?"

"Yes." Something unlocked inside her as she said it. A door, a window—something.

The Chair exhaled. "Alright. Make sure to tell the attorneys you've worked with. In person."

She hadn't thought about that.

He was right.

Ember nodded. "Thank you," and walked out.

Her supervising partner was first. His office smelled like old leather and coffee. He sat behind a desk stacked with contracts, his reading glasses perched low on his nose.

Ember told him that she was leaving the firm, and he gave her a slow nod, as if considering something he wasn't saying.

"You gotta like what you do," he said finally.

That was it. No argument. No advice.

Next was a partner who had mentored her when she summered at the firm. As Ember entered his office, she noticed that his usual sharpness was softened by the scruff on his face, a look somewhere between exhaustion and carelessness. After she told him, he looked at her, really looked at her, and then reached out his hand. "Good for you." Ember shook his hand, the warmth of his palm grounding her.

Then came Rachel—her mentor—who barely looked up from the stack of papers on her desk.

After that, Ember made her way to Jon's office. The moment she stepped inside, something shifted. "I'm leaving law," Ember said. "Looking for work on the business side."

Jon leaned back, crossing his arms. "Congratulations."

Ember frowned. "I don't know what you're congratulating me for. I don't have another job lined up yet."

Jon didn't hesitate. "You're getting out. Congratulations. It's the right move. I'm envious."

Ember blinked.

Jon. Senior Partner. One of the most powerful attorneys in the department.

And he was envious.

A crack formed in her understanding of this place.

By the time she reached David's office, she had stopped expecting anything surprising. He looked up from his desk, tilting his head.

"You're leaving?"

"I am."

A slow grin spread across his face. "Damn."

"What?"

He leaned back. "Are you hiring?"

"Not yet," Ember laughed.

David shook his head, still grinning. "The door's open if you ever change your mind."

"I don't think I will." Ember said.

His grin didn't fade. "I don't think so either."

As Ember walked down the hallway, she felt it fall away.

The pretense.

The performance.

The lie.

She stepped into the elevator, and the doors slid shut.

She exhaled.

She was free.

CHAPTER 50

UNWRITTEN

Ember paced her small apartment, her cell phone pressed tightly to her ear, eyes wide with exhilaration. "I did it, Brendan! Can you believe it? I actually did it!"

"Slow down," Brendan said, a smile in his voice. "Did what, exactly?"

Ember laughed as she leaned against her kitchen counter, gripping its edge for support. "I put in my notice. I'm officially done at the firm. It's over."

On the other end of the phone, Brendan let out a deliberate, astonished breath. "Wow, Ember. That's huge." A pause. Then his tone shifted, more cautious now. "But, what are you going to do now? I know how miserable you've been, but I also know we both have six-figure law school debt to consider."

"Don't worry," Ember reassured him, pulling herself upright and lifting her chin with newfound determination. "I have a plan."

Brendan chuckled, familiar with her confident tone. "You always do," he said. "But seriously, aren't you even a little scared?"

She hesitated. Her gaze shifting toward the window and the city lights beyond, then shook her head even though Brendan couldn't see it. "Maybe a little. But honestly? Staying was scarier. I had to do something drastic to save myself."

Brendan sighed, a note of admiration mingling with envy. "I'm probably not far behind you. Just need to figure out my own exit strategy first."

"Well, hurry up," Ember teased. "Alright, I should go—I have an interview tomorrow, and I need to prep."

"An interview already? You really don't waste time, do you?" Brendan joked.

"Not anymore," she laughed. "I'll let you know how it goes."

"You better. Good luck," he said. "You've got this."

"Thanks, Brendan." Ember ended the call, placing the phone carefully on the counter.

Relief washed over her. She stood still, as her reflection stared back from the darkened window, her eyes alight with possibility.

Tomorrow's interview wasn't really an interview—it was her first pitch, a chance to sell her vision to the world.

She took a deep breath, straightened her shoulders, and smiled.

This was her moment to write her future.

CHAPTER 51

THE PITCH

The conference room was sleek, its floor-to-ceiling windows overlooking the city skyline. Sunlight reflected off glass towers in the distance, but inside, everything was still. Measured. A long glass table stretched between Ember and the investors—five of them, all sharply dressed, all watching her with the kind of quiet intensity that came with years of making high-stakes decisions.

She had seen rooms like this before. Had worked in them. Had watched million-dollar deals take shape over contracts filled with language so dense it crushed the air out of the room.

But this was different.

This time, she was on the other side of the table.

She adjusted the small remote in her hand, steadied herself, and took a breath.

Then she began.

"Imagine if there were a place where you could fully understand the implications of your choices."

A few eyebrows lifted.

"For this choice, you will battle insecurity. For that choice, ego. And you don't just think about it—you *feel* it. You experience who in your life it affects. You see the trajectory unfold. And then, you decide."

She had their attention and clicked to the next slide.

"Every day, people make life-altering decisions—career changes, family choices, moves across the world—without truly understanding what they're stepping into. Traditional mindfulness tools—meditation, yoga, coaching—are powerful, but they require faith. They require belief before someone experiences the outcome. And in a world of instant gratification, that's a hard sell."

One of the investors, a woman in a crisp navy suit, folded her hands and leaned forward. "You're talking about a predictive model for life choices?"

Ember shook her head. "I'm talking about simulated experience. We already know the answer to so many of life's questions. We just don't have a way to *feel* them before we decide. What if we offered a way to step inside your life's choices before making them?"

She let that sink in for a moment.

The energy in the room shifted.

She could feel it now—*curiosity.* And she took the plunge.

She clicked on the next slide which showed clean white letters on a black background: The Solution.

"Resonance VR is a fully immersive experience where users can step inside their own decisions before they make them. They don't just think about their choices—they feel them. They experience the trade-offs firsthand, in a safe virtual environment.

Pilots don't fly without spending hours in a simulator—so why do we approach life's biggest decisions with less preparation?"

The click of a pen. A notepad flipped over.

They were listening.

"Right now, students commit to law school before ever stepping foot inside a firm. Couples make life-changing decisions about marriage and children without truly knowing the weight of those choices. Employees take jobs in cities they've never lived in. These are not new decisions. But the way we make them is outdated. There's no structured space to explore life's biggest choices. That changes today."

She moved through the deck, feeling the room lean in as she spoke.

The Market. $115 billion industry, growing at nearly 9% annually. A consumer base that was already primed for this—millions of people looking for deeper meaning, clarity, direction.

Traction. Early pilots. Beta partnerships. Testimonials from users who had already stepped inside Resonance VR and come out the other side changed.

Then...the ask.

"$25 million to scale product development, expand partnerships, and bring Resonance VR to market at a global level."

No one flinched, so Ember continued.

"In closing, we have the opportunity to take the emerging movement of yoga, meditation, and self-awareness—and give it a *technological revolution*. What if the same immersive engagement that makes people lose themselves in gaming could be used to help them *find* themselves instead?"

"Who are your buyers?" one investor asked.

Ember smiled.

"We start where transformation is already happening—wellness retreats, yoga studios, universities. We work with institutions that are already guiding people through life's big decisions. Resonance VR doesn't replace mindfulness—it makes it accessible."

Another investor leaned forward. "And the business model?"

"B2C subscription for individuals. B2B partnerships for corporate wellness programs, universities, and retreats. The technology isn't just a tool—it's an experience people will seek out. Once they step inside it, they *get* it."

More questions. More clarifications. And then—the pause. The moment where she could feel it hanging in the air, the weight of consideration, of possibility.

The office felt bigger now. The moment had stretched it into something else.

Ember stood at the front of the room, her hands steady at her sides, feet planted firm. The investors—five of them, all seasoned, all calculating—watched her in silence.

She had answered every question. Some meant to poke holes in her pitch, to test for weaknesses. Others were just curiosity wrapped in skepticism.

She had met each one head-on.

Now, it seemed there was only one person left to speak.

The oldest investor at the table—a man in his seventies, silver-haired and quiet—shifted in his seat.

"You keep saying once they step inside, they get it," he said. "That it's something you feel." He went quiet for a moment, letting the words hang in the air. "So why are we still sitting here talking about it?"

A murmur of agreement. A glance exchanged between two others.

Ember felt her pulse quicken. This was it. No more explaining. No more slides. It was time to show them.

Ember set the headset in front of him.

"This isn't a game," she said, her voice calm and even. "It's your decision of what to do with your one precious life."

He picked up the headset, adjusted it over his silver hair, and settled into his chair.

Ember pressed start. The massive screen behind Ember showed the other investors what he saw.

•◆•

A corner office—rich mahogany desk, city skyline stretching beyond the glass.

A place he had spent decades in.

And yet, something was off.

The investor's fingers curled on the table in front of him. He sat still, but his jaw shifted.

A woman—someone younger, someone new—stood behind the desk, speaking to a colleague. Neither of them noticed him.

A hollow feeling crept inside him.

He turned and saw that the plaque that had once carried his name was gone.

His throat tightened.

The office melted away.

Now, he was in his own home—but it felt too big.

A leather chair he had sat in for years. A book he had started but never finished. The television playing in the background, something he wasn't really watching.

It was quiet.

A silence that wasn't peaceful. A silence that was waiting.

A silence that stretched through the walls, through time.

He shifted in his seat in real life, his fingers twitching against the armrest.

Then—

Laughter.

A piercing, golden sound that broke the quiet apart.

He turned again.

A backyard.

The light was different here—warmer, softer, filled with motion.

And in it, his grandchildren.

His lips parted.

A little girl with wild curls tugged at his hand, her small fingers warm against his. "Come on, Grandpa!" she giggled, pulling him down into the grass.

A boy, no older than six, held out a paper airplane, waiting for him to take it.

The investor's breathing changed.

His chest rose, then fell—slower, fuller.

His hand lifted to take the airplane. And the second his fingers closed around it, the simulation ended.

•◆•

He pulled off the headset. For a long moment, he didn't say anything. Didn't move. His eyes were unfocused, adjusting. His breathing wasn't the same as before.

Ember intentionally didn't speak. She let him sit in it. Let the moment land.

The old man exhaled and ran a hand over his face.

"I almost missed it," he said. Solemn.

The air in the room changed.

The other investors had just watched the shift happen in real time.

He sat back in his chair, nodding slowly. Then, looked around the table, and with a nod, he said: "We're in. With one caveat."

Ember lifted an eyebrow. "What's that?"

His eyes sparkled.

"The tagline." He folded his hands. "It has to be: *Feel Something*."

Ember smiled and nodded. "That's right. You're right—it does."

By the time she stepped out of the building, the city felt different. Crisper. Louder. Like she could hear every car horn, every distant voice, every hum of electricity in the air.

The meeting had ended with handshakes, numbers exchanged, next steps locked in.

This was real.

The weight of it hit her all at once. Not heavy. Expansive. Like the moment when you finally take the deepest breath you didn't know you needed. She threw her head back and laughed, the sound light.

And finally, she realized that she wasn't waiting for her life to start anymore.

It had just launched.

She practically floated down the steps, the adrenaline still coursing through her, her heartbeat matching the rhythm of something bigger. When she saw him.

Derek.

He was leaning against a lamppost, arms crossed, watching her with the same beaming smile he had the first time they met in the cave in Resonance. Frank sat at his feet, tail thumping against the pavement.

The second Ember saw them, the flood of reality hit her all over again. She laughed a real, unrestrained laugh as she hurried towards them. "They said yes."

Derek pushed off the post, his grin widening. "Of course they did."

Ember shook her head. "No, you don't get it. They really said yes. This is happening."

Derek stepped closer, studying her face. "I get it." His voice softened. "I always got it. They just needed to see what I already saw."

This man—this infuriating, brilliant, loyal man—had been there when Resonance VR was just an idea. He had helped her build the prototype, had stood in the background while she fought for it. He believed in this before the investors ever did.

Ember met Derek's gaze. "Thank you," she whispered. "For helping me build this. For…" She exhaled. "For seeing it when it was just an idea in my head."

"Anytime." Derek held her stare, his expression shifting into something deeper.

The city moved around them, the world carrying on.

But in that moment—

Nothing else existed.

Ember reached for him, and Derek didn't hesitate.

He pulled her in.

And when they kissed, the world around them exploded into color.

CHAPTER 52

THE TIDE

The café was sleek and modern, a place where attorneys and executives met when they needed privacy but not distance. The kind of place where decisions were made quietly, over espressos and unspoken hierarchies.

Sunlight filtered through the floor-to-ceiling windows, casting sharp reflections on the polished marble tabletops. The hum of conversation was low but constant, the sound of deals being made, careers being shaped.

Ember sat across from David, the heir apparent at her old firm. A rising star with the right last name and a string of high-profile wins, he was already being groomed for leadership. He looked exactly as she remembered—precisely tailored, effortlessly composed, the weight of the firm's legacy stitched into every careful movement.

But there was something in his expression she hadn't seen before.

Curiosity.

He stirred his coffee once, and set the spoon down. "I wanted to understand why you left." He paused. "I've seen plenty of female attorneys leave when the horrible conflict between biology and this job catches up to them." He exhaled through his nose. "But that's not why you left." He studied her. "So, what went wrong?"

Ember inhaled, and instinctively pressed her palms to her chest. And to her own surprise, she answered: "I felt my light dimming," she said. "And I promised myself I would never let that happen."

She braced for an eyeroll, a smirk, a dismissive comment about how poetic she had become.

But David just nodded. "Well," he murmured, "that happened quickly."

"Yes," Ember agreed. "It did."

They sat in silence.

Outside, people moved with purpose, in suits and heels, eyes locked on their phones, their paths fixed. She had walked among them once, felt the same urgency.

For the first time, she saw it from the outside.

And she knew she wasn't supposed to be there anymore.

David pressed his hands against the table as he stood. His voice was quieter this time, almost thoughtful. "You know what, Ember? Good for you. Damn. Good for you." he said.

She lifted her eyes to him. And for the first time, it seemed that he saw her too—not the associate he once mentored, not the attorney he had expected to keep, but the person she had become. David gave a small nod, their conversation settling into its natural conclusion. He walked out of the café and disappeared into the city's current, another figure in a tide that no longer pulled her under.

CHAPTER 53

FIGHT FOR YOUR LIGHT

Ember sat there for a long time, fingers resting against the table, feeling the weight of everything she had left behind meeting the weightlessness of what lay ahead.

It had all happened so quickly.

But it had happened exactly as it was meant to.

She stood, stepping out into golden afternoon light, into her life, into the unknown.

She no longer had to remind herself to breathe. That part was easy now.

But keeping her light—that would take something more.

Because the world would try to dim it.

It always did.

And that was what she would have to remember.

ACKNOWLEDGEMENTS

Writing this book was not a solo endeavor. I'm deeply grateful to those who helped shape, support, and challenge me along the way.

To my son—thank you for creating the urgency to get this book into the world, and for reminding me every day what matters.

To my husband, who grounds me in reality.

To my mother, for her unwavering spirit.

To my father, who taught me how to challenge the rules.

To David Roper, for being both a coach and a mentor throughout this journey. Your insights into dialogue, character development, and conflict brought the story to life. You identified pivotal elements—like the title and cover—that I couldn't see as unique while immersed in the process. Your brilliance is inspiring.

To Prana Power Yoga and its teachers—your training marked a before and after in my life. I quit my law firm job during it and found a new path.

To the musicians who cracked me open, inspired my words, and made me brave enough to share them:

- Beautiful Chorus, Cyril, DJ Taz Rashid, Jack Garratt, KR3TURE, Rising Appalachia, Sol Rising, The Human Experience, and Trevor Hall—for sounds that feel like home.

- Charlotte Plank, Evanescence, Godsmack, Limp Bizkit, Muse, and Radiohead—for the pulse of rage and rebellion.
- Dua Lipa, heylucas, Keala Settle, Natasha Bedingfield, and Rachel Platten—for the courage to be seen.

To Disney, for Ursula the sea witch who captured Ariel's voice. That's how I felt as a law firm associate. Such a poor unfortunate soul.

To Ingrid Hillinger, who taught me how to think and write.

To Andrea Hurst, who read an early manuscript and gave me four years of homework. I did it.

To Jess King, for coaching me through fear.

To Jason Barnwell, for helping me to see myself clearly.

To Kathryn Trotter, for helping me see my book clearly.

To Marblehead Yoga Loft and Gurdeep Bhogal's Yin & Reiki classes—thank you for being a place of refuge.

To Renew Yoga—thank you for the cleansing flow and the radiance it revealed.

To the group of women who showed up in Marblehead for a narrated screening of Soul Toll—the first people to experience this story aloud. Your grace and curiosity made it real.

To early influencers who guided me to stand out like Dorie Clarke, Shama Hyder, and Marie Forleo.

To early champions like Anna Lozynski, Bjarne Tellmann, Carly Gioia, Cat Moon, Cynthia Shoss, Jennifer Riggs, Jihan Hassan Merlin, Nicola Shaver, Sian O'Neil, and others who engaged in surveys and hyped this book on social media before it had a cover.

To creators who moved me from afar, especially Michael Singer for *The Untethered Soul*, and Sarah Blondin for *Live Awake*.

And to whatever force it was that insisted this book be written—thank you.

I'm finally free.